THE REVELRY

KATHERINE WEBBER

WALKER
BOOKS

First published in Great Britain 2022 by Walker Books Ltd
87 Vauxhall Walk, London SE11 5HJ

2 4 6 8 10 9 7 5 3 1

Text © 2022 Katherine Webber
Cover illustration by Leo Nickolls

This book has been typeset in Fairfield LH, Bauer Bodoni, Open Sans,
Linotype Zapfino, Madelyn Doodles Fill and Atmosphere

Printed and bound by CPI Group (UK) Ltd, Croydon CR0 4YY

British Library Cataloguing in Publication Data:
a catalogue record for this book is available from the British Library

ISBN 978-1-4063-8844-2

www.walker.co.uk

MIX
Paper from
responsible sources
FSC® C171272

For Fay and Janou, my oldest friends.
Thank you for a childhood spent wandering
in the woods of our imagination.

Seven trees for seven wishes
Seven hearts for seven kisses
Seven deaths for seven dreams
Seven stitches in seven seams
Try to jump from six to eight
Because seven is where you'll meet your fate

– UNKNOWN, *The Fate of Seven*

One

I am a girl from Ember Grove, and these are my woods.

I grew up with the dark woods as my playground. Hide-and-seek among the trees. Play pretend on the lake shore. I know every root and bramble, thorn and stone.

But there are parts of the woods I would never go to alone.

Tonight is different.

Tonight is the Revelry.

Tonight the woods are ours for the taking.

The Revelry is more than a party: the Revelry can change your entire future.

Ember Grove is a town fuelled by rumours and superstition. Local myths and half-forgotten fables – and the Revelry is the most important of them all.

A night to change your destiny.

To find out if Ember Grove will let you go … or keep hold of you forever.

Not me. I, Bitsy Clark, am going to get out of Ember Grove. Like my brother Harvey did. He's at Cobalt University down the coast. We don't hear from him much – when people leave, they don't tend to come back, even to visit – but I think he's happy down at Cobalt.

Who wouldn't be happier away from our small town, where secrets and success battle for space? Where the woods listen to every whisper?

Where one party can change everything?

The events of each Revelry are a closely guarded secret, kept between that year's attendees. Nobody talks about their Revelry, there are no photos, no official guest list, no proof of anything that happens. Of course, whispers slither out, rumours spread and stories from Revelries gone by turn to local legend. Like one year, supposedly flowers bloomed between kissing couples all night long. And then everyone started to believe that when you have your first kiss, and it is with someone who likes you back, something green will grow. Amy agonized over this one, because she lives in an apartment with no green space at all, but then, and I'm telling the truth, the week after she kissed Mark Lee during spin the bottle, a little dandelion sprout appeared on her windowsill. A Revelry rule that spilled out into town and lasted longer than one night. It happens all the time.

The Revelry is meant to be just for the graduating high-school class, no exceptions. It happens every year, almost by magic, all the adults turning the other way, as if it's not for them to worry about. Everyone in town knows when it is, and even though there are whispers of what *could* happen, what *has* happened in years past, what *will* happen, nobody tries to stop it. Trying to stop the Revelry would be like trying to stop the seasons from changing. It is just as much a part of Ember Grove as the woods themselves.

It isn't my year. I'm sixteen and shouldn't be going for another two summers...

Apparently Amy has other plans.

Amy's my best friend. She has been since she moved to Ember Grove eight years ago, when we were eight, and our own Revelry felt like a lifetime away.

Just like Ember Grove doesn't like to let go of its inhabitants, it doesn't always welcome new ones. But I saw this new girl, standing in front of the class with her head high and secrets clutched tight to her chest, and I knew I wanted to be her friend. So I grabbed her hand and I pulled her deep into Ember Grove. She'd never belong like I did, of course, but I did everything I could. I showed her the woods, showed her the town, made sure she felt welcome. Made her an Ember Grove girl in everything but birth.

The night I told her about the Revelry we were sleeping in a tent out in the apple orchard behind my house. The only light was from my little flashlight, propped up at the front of the tent by our feet. It was cold, colder than it should have been for a summer night.

I told her about the Revelry the same way I told her the story about Mrs Glen found dead on her porch, surrounded by nine snowy white owls. In a hushed voice, awe and fear mingling in my voice, I told her everything I knew about the magic party in the woods, which wasn't much, just stolen whispers and local legends.

And Amy became obsessed.

Ever since, she's tried to find out what day it falls, exactly where it happens – *what* happens. All we know is that it's near the end of summer, before the new school year starts.

And that it's in the woods.

Once, when we were around nine, and still having sleepovers in the tent in the apple orchard, we saw people stumbling out of the woods at dawn. Two girls were laughing, high-pitched almost hysterical giggles, but one boy, I could have sworn he was bleeding. And the strangest thing was they were all wearing wings. Costume wings, the kind you slip over your shoulders and the fake feathers moult in minutes, but as they came out of the woods, for a moment I thought those wings were real. And we knew, we *knew* they had come from the Revelry. We watched them in silence, waiting for a hint, a clue to what had happened.

But they didn't notice us at all.

A girl disappeared that year. Florence Lonsdale. She went to the Revelry and never came back. But nobody talked about where she went. About what had happened. Or if they did, we never heard a word.

The next year, the Revelry happened again. Like it always does.

And this year, Amy is determined to go. She's been set on this since the seasons changed, even though it isn't our Revelry, even though she *knows* that wanting to isn't enough.

I keep telling her this and I'm ready to tell her again, but then she pulls out her trump card.

"I've got an invite." Amy holds out a Revelry invitation. It's the first time, ever, that she's known something about Ember Grove before me.

"That isn't how they do it," I scoff. But I'm not sure. Maybe it is. I'm dismissive on purpose. I know more about the Revelry than Amy, surely. But maybe I'm wrong: maybe this is how it is done.

"We might as well try," she says, giving me a sly smile. "Unless you're scared."

"I'm not scared," I say quickly. "But someone's playing a prank on you. No way is that legit." But still. I take the invite out of her hands like it might go up in flames at any moment.

It's a small white card cut from thick, expensive paper that smells like the woods. And embossed on one side it says:

Your Presence is Requested at

THE REVELRY

Dress code: Decadent Dionysian Bacchanalia

Location: Lake Lost

Time: Midnight

And on the other side tomorrow's date is handwritten in gold ink, as fine as lace. I delicately run my fingers over the writing, as if I could magically tell who had written it by mere touch. My fingers come away wet and flecked with gold: the ink still isn't dry. My heart begins to hammer in my chest.

"Where did you even find this?" I say. "Did you write the date?"

Amy's grin widened. "Of course I didn't write the date. And as for the invite itself, I found it."

"Where?" I demand.

"By the Founder's Fountain," she says. And I don't know why, but I shudder.

"Even if it is real, it isn't for you," I counter. "It isn't for us. Invite or no invite, we can't go." The very thought makes my skin feel tight. If you find a set of keys on a lawn, you don't get to let yourself into a stranger's house, sleep in their bed and put on their clothes.

"Can't we?" Amy deftly grabs the card out of my hands and waves it in front of my eyes like a magician doing a trick. "Come on, Bits. It's the Revelry."

Exactly I want to say. She doesn't get what a big deal it is to sneak into a Revelry that isn't your own. What the consequences might be – even *I* don't know what could happen.

There are so many unwritten rules that thread their way through the lives of everyone in Ember Grove. Pull at one and everything might unravel...

But. The idea has sunk its teeth into me – and Amy has a magic of her own, a way of always getting what she wants. Whether I go or not, Amy will – and there is no way I'd let her go without me. I'd die of jealousy if she experienced a Revelry before I did.

I let out a long breath, a smile spreading across my face.

Amy knows she has me then. "It's time for some new traditions in Ember Grove," she says. And her smile matches mine.

Two

We don't have much time to prepare.

If it was *our* Revelry, the one meant for us, we would have had days, weeks, to get ready.

But Amy jumps into action. I'm not exactly sure what a dress code of "Dionysian Bacchanalia" even means, but Amy does.

"Think togas. But like *decadent* togas. Greek gods and goddesses. That kind of thing," she says as she leaves my house, invitation in hand. "I've got this covered."

Like she's been waiting years for this, which I guess in some ways she has.

We decide to get ready at Amy's apartment because her Aunt Lily is working the night shift at the hospital so she won't know what we're getting up to. My parents trust me, but even they would be suspicious if we waltzed out of the front door at midnight dressed like Greeks or Romans or whatever we are supposed to be tonight.

My mom's surprised enough that I'm sleeping over at Amy's. She knows I don't like staying over at Amy's apartment.

It isn't because Amy's apartment is small and dark, and the lighting is terrible for getting ready. Or that it is almost always cold. Or that she lives right at the top of the main road in town, where you can always hear the traffic, even with the windows closed.

I don't like Amy's apartment because I'm sure it's haunted.

She lives in the old hospital. It isn't a hospital any more, of course – it was turned into a series of apartments years ago. It's next door to the new hospital, where Amy's Aunt Lily works.

When we were younger, we would try to figure out what her room used to be.

"Maybe babies were born in here," I'd say, cradling a doll to my chest.

"Or maybe this is where they cut people open!" Amy would counter, brandishing a pencil like a scalpel.

Neither of us ever said what must have been on both our minds.

Maybe somebody died in this room.

I try not to think of this when I step into her building, where the air grows stale and the street noise fades as the door swings shut. The corridors are always empty and I pull my coat more closely around me as I hurry through them.

But when Amy opens her door, she's already dressed. I immediately grin, because she's taken the theme and put her own spin on it, like she always does. She's in a colourful toga that she must have tie-dyed herself. The colours are a swirl of vibrant pinks and blues that complement her bright purple hair and golden skin. Even in the harsh light of her apartment, she's glowing, the way she always is.

She grabs my arm and pulls me inside, closing the door to the draughty hall and locking it.

As if locking it could keep out anything that wanted to get in.

I follow her into her room, with its narrow bed and small, square window. It's nothing like my room, with its skylights and floor-to-ceiling mirrored closets and bed covered with overstuffed pillows. Despite how I feel about Amy's apartment, I've slept here dozens and dozens of times over the years. When we were small, we fitted in the bed no problem, and used to sleep head to toe, giggling as we tickled each other's feet. And as we grew, we still managed to squeeze in together, falling asleep curled up like sisters, or cats.

Amy's aunt isn't a hugger like my parents. The first time I gave Amy a hug, she'd only been in Ember Grove for about a month, but we'd spent most days together after school. And then one day, she started crying at lunch. She'd just found out that she was staying with Aunt Lily for the foreseeable future, not just for a few weeks like she'd thought, and I did what I always did when someone was upset: I gave her a hug. But instead of hugging me back, she went stiff all over, like she didn't know what to do.

That was years ago, though. Since then there have been countless nights sharing a bed, fixing each other's hair, doing each other's make-up, snuggled up watching a movie. We're always draped over each other – and Amy's affectionate with everyone now, especially her theatre friends. But I'll always remember that I was the one who brought her out of her shell all those years ago. I was the one that she needed.

"You look great," I say, and I mean it. She's done dramatic eye make-up with purple shadow the same shade as her hair and thick black liner that goes up in perfect winged tips, accentuating her dark eyes. Her lips are pink. Bright and attention-grabbing and high fashion all at once.

"It's not too much?" she says, spinning in a slow, dramatic circle.

I laugh. "Too much is your signature."

"Purple hair is my signature."

"This week."

Amy rolls her eyes but she smiles. "Fair."

Today Amy's hair is an almost electric purple, like bubblegum pink mixed with neon blue. Last Christmas it was soft lavender. And before that, it was the blue of peacock feathers.

Sometimes I feel a little dull with my boring blonde hair. Always the same shade, always the same style. I know Amy would dye it for me if I asked, but I'm too chicken. What if I hated it? Amy never seems to worry about that; she dives in first, worries afterwards.

Like she's doing tonight…

Amy never had this confidence when we were younger. It kind of grew over time. And meanwhile, I feel like I stayed the same. I mean, of course I grew. God knows I *grew*. I'm almost six feet now. Amy and my mom are always telling me I should celebrate my height, but I always feel a little out of place. When I was ten, I was so sure of myself. Now that I'm sixteen, I feel like my confidence hasn't grown with me.

Tonight I'll have to borrow a little of my best friend's self-belief – something Amy is always happy to share. She believes in me like no one else. It's one of the things I love most about her.

"Enough about me." She flashes me a wide smile. "Time to get you all dolled up"

"If you insist," I say, grinning back at her. She knows I love it when she helps me get ready. She leans back to appraise me.

"We'll start with your hair. You, my dear Bitsy, are going to look like a Greek goddess," she says. "Here, sit on the floor." I oblige, sitting on the worn carpet, and she sits on the bed behind me. I can feel her fingers knotting and twisting in my hair, pulling tightly on one section and then starting again somewhere else. "Almost done," she says around a mouthful of hair pins. "Let me just touch up your make-up."

"I'm already wearing make-up." I put on mascara and blusher before I came over.

"Bitsy, you're wearing everyday Bitsy make-up. Tonight, you're a goddess, remember? Now close your eyes."

"Don't do too much," I say. What I mean is, *don't make me look like you*. It looks amazing on Amy, genuinely, but I'd look and feel like a clown doll.

"I know what you like. Don't worry."

22

I close my eyes and relax as Amy deftly applies eyeshadow and shimmer and lipstick. Amy has spent years doing her own make-up for all the plays and musicals she's in, and she's now so good she could probably do it professionally.

"Don't worry," she murmurs. "I'm going for a Helen of Troy vibe. You are going to love it. Dewy, radiant, a face to launch a thousand ships, all of that."

I snort. "Amy, you're good with make-up, but you aren't *that* good."

"Hush, ye of little faith. Hold on … one more second… Ta-da!"

When I open my eyes and look at my reflection in the mirror, I almost don't recognize the person staring back at me. Amy has done something with my eyes to make the blue of my irises pop in a way they never have before, and I don't know how she transformed my round cheeks into sculpted cheekbones you could ski off, but she has. Some of my hair is tied up in complicated braids, but the rest tumbles down my back in golden curls. I never knew my hair could look like this. I never knew *I* could look like this.

"Well?" she asks, beaming at me.

"You have magic in your fingertips," I say. "Only you could make me look like this."

"I had a good canvas to work with," she says. "Now, time for your toga!" She picks up what looks like a blue sheet from her bed.

I realize it *is* a blue sheet. She must see my expression because she laughs. "It was the best I could do at such short notice." She helps me tie the toga on, and when we go into the bathroom to get a better look, I can see how it all comes together. I look like someone who does exciting things, who has secrets, and always leaves people wanting more. And I like that. We lean against each other and grin. I want to take a picture, to remember this moment, to remember not only how I looked but how I felt, but...

Amy doesn't suggest it and neither do I. Revelry rules apply to the whole night and there's no point breaking more of them than necessary.

"And for the final touch..." Amy reaches into her bag and pulls out two matching gold circlets. She places one on my head, and one on her own.

"Now we're ready," she says.

Even though I know I'm just wearing a cheap blue sheet wrapped around me, I feel regal. Powerful. Almost magical.

Exactly as I always imagined I'd feel going to the Revelry.

But then I get a sharp stab of apprehension.

24

"Maybe this isn't a good idea," I say. Because it isn't our year. It isn't *for* us. I don't know what will happen when we get there. If we'll even be able to find our way there in the woods. Or worse, if we do find our way there and we're punished for going to a Revelry that isn't our own.

"You're right." Relief floods through me when I hear Amy say this as she adjusts her toga. But then, "It isn't a good idea – it's a *great* idea. Besides, we can't be the first people to ever sneak into a Revelry. We just haven't heard about the others because, you know, *secrecy*."

Perhaps she's right. Perhaps I'm letting all the mystery and tradition get to me. It's just a party, after all.

Just a party, I repeat to myself as we do final checks on our make-up and hair. Right before we leave, Amy goes to the kitchen and comes back with a dusty bottle of red wine. She holds it aloft. "Liquid courage?"

I shake my head. I don't like drinking, don't like losing any sense of control. Things are strange enough in Ember Grove – I like to keep my wits about me. I know Amy drinks with her Drama Club friends on the final night of their performances, but I'm definitely not letting her drink tonight.

"No way," I say. "And none for you either. We need to be sharp if we're going to find our way there."

Amy sighs. "I suppose you're right." She comes back empty-handed, but with a renewed sense of excitement. "I have an idea. I think we should leave here right on midnight. Like reverse Cinderellas."

I glance at the clock. It is already eleven; an hour isn't too long to wait. And the idea appeals to me. So we sit on her bed in our togas and flip through old yearbooks, laughing at how young we used to look. Then, right before midnight, we count down, almost like it is New Year's Eve, and right before the day ends, we open up the door, and, giggling, hurry out of the old hospital. As soon as we're outside, I breathe in deeply, revelling in the fresh night air.

We link arms and stroll down Main Street, passing Lee's Bakery, the post office and the old movie theatre and arcade that are still in business somehow. The lights are off in every building. And we see nobody, unless you count the Ember Grove Founder's statue, bursting proudly from its fountain base.

The statue is so old its features have been worn away over time, and now it's a faceless statue of a person growing out of a tree trunk, holding their cupped hands out in front of them. In their hands is a carving of a flame that sometimes looks like it is flickering, even though it's made of stone.

"We should have brought a penny to toss in for good luck," I say. My voice is light, but I mean it and on instinct I reach for one, but my toga doesn't have pockets.

"I swear, all of your allowance when we were kids went to this damn statue," says Amy. "I'll throw in a penny tomorrow for you, OK?"

"I don't think it works like that."

Amy snorts. "I don't think it works at all." Of course she doesn't – she never has. "Anyway, tonight, we make our own luck."

"Right," I say. But I'm careful not to look at the Founder as we pass their silent beckoning.

At the end of Main Street is the big brick library that stands sentinel. Beyond that the woods.

Here, Amy pauses. We both know that once we go into the woods, we won't be turning back. The trees loom over us, swaying in the wind, and I can't tell if they are beckoning us to come closer, or warning us to stay away.

"Come on," I say, growing bold in the moment. After all, I'm a girl from Ember Grove. These are my woods, Revelry or no Revelry.

"Wait," says Amy. "We almost forgot." And I know what she's going to do. She tugs two strands of her hair from her head, and I do the same, and hand them to her.

"So we don't lose each other," I say, with a smile. She quickly twists the hairs together, making two delicate rings, and we tie them on our index fingers, knotting them to make sure they stay on.

We've been doing it for years, tying ourselves together with our hair when we go into the woods, so we can always find our way back to each other.

For all of her teasing about the traditions and myths of Ember Grove, this is one superstition that Amy takes seriously.

I do too.

Three

There is a lake in the middle of the woods that isn't always there.

It doesn't matter how often you've been there, how well you think you know the way, sometimes you can't ever find it.

It's called Lake Lost.

This is where the Revelry is. On the shore of Lake Lost, deep in the woods of Ember Grove.

We'll either find it, or we won't. And I know in my heart that if we truly aren't meant to be at this Revelry, we'll never find the lake.

The woods are dark.

Amy uses her phone as a flashlight. It's the only thing it's good for – there's no reception and the maps are meaningless when all you can see are trees. I haven't even brought mine. I left it back at her apartment. At first the trail is well-travelled and obvious, but the deeper we go, the narrower it grows. Until there isn't a trail at all.

"Which way do you think we go?" I hear a hint of nerves in Amy's voice.

The trees around us begin to change, shifting from sturdy cedar and familiar pine, to trees I don't usually see, like pale birch and towering eucalyptus. But this doesn't frighten me. It makes me think we must be getting closer.

Branches scratch my bare shoulders and twigs snap underfoot. The moonlight filters down through the leaves above us, making the white birches glow in the night and the pink and green of the peeling eucalyptus trunks look otherworldly. I blink and the moonlight shifts, and the tree I was just looking at has disappeared. My senses are playing tricks on me.

The air is growing heavier around us, like we're walking through an invisible fog. My skin is damp with a mist I can't see, and the earth beneath my feet begins to feel spongy. The way that fresh dirt feels when it has been tilled. It's strange, and unsettling, but not unpleasant.

I have the very particular sensation of being watched, but that isn't unusual in the woods. Legend says the trees themselves pay attention. Especially on the night of the Revelry.

Suddenly, for the first time in my entire life, I'm truly lost in my woods. Even if we wanted to turn around now and find our way out, I don't know if we could.

We have to find the lake.

We silently wind our way through the trees, our togas catching on the occasional branch, before I hear it: the gentle lapping of water against the shore somewhere up ahead. We're close. I start to walk faster, eager to get there, my heart flapping in my chest like a bird beating against a window.

I'm not watching where I'm going and suddenly there's a crunch and a quiet squeak beneath my foot. I feel the wrongness of what I've stepped on reverberate through the thin soles of my silver sandals and up my leg.

Something small and delicate has cracked beneath me.

I don't want to look.

"What is it?" says Amy, because I've stopped so suddenly.

"I … I think I stepped on something," I whisper. I don't want to lift my foot to see what it is. I feel dizzy, and a little sick.

Amy scrunches her face, not getting it. "Yeah, like leaves or sticks, Bits."

"Not leaves," I say, trembling now. "Can you help me look?"

I slowly raise my foot as Amy points the light down.

There, nestled in the imprint of my sandal, is a tiny baby bird. Its wings are splayed, and it is very clearly dead. Its feathers are grey and fluffy, and its little beak is open, like it's trying to speak.

Its eyes are open too.

I stagger back, bile rising along with the horror.

"Oh, man," says Amy, turning the light on her phone off, and drenching us in welcome darkness. "Poor baby bird."

"What was it doing on the ground?" I say, bracing myself on the tree next to me. "At night?"

"It was probably already dead," says Amy, but she doesn't sound very convincing. "It must have fallen out of its nest. Broke its neck." She strokes my arm. "It wasn't your fault."

I remember the soft pressure I felt under my foot, right before the crunch, and the small squeak. I know that I killed it.

"We should get going. We're almost there," says Amy gently, tugging on my arm.

All my excitement and apprehension about tonight, about the Revelry, has coalesced into this moment. I can't see anything but the broken bird on the ground in front of me.

You don't grow up in Ember Grove without believing in omens, in the weight of warnings.

We shouldn't be here.

This isn't our night.

This isn't our Revelry.

But I can hear the lake up ahead, and the sound is pulling me towards it. I glance back down at the baby bird, and clasp my hand over my mouth again.

Amy looks at me and sighs with resignation. And for a moment I think she's going to say that we should turn back, even though I don't know how we'll find our way out of the woods now, but then she squats down, and digs a little hole in the dirt, then, using the bottom of her tie-dyed toga, she scoops up the broken bird and gently puts it in the makeshift grave.

The bird is still dead, but at least now it is buried. I sigh in relief, and swear I hear the woods do the same.

"Thank you," I whisper. And I'm grateful, I am, but I also wish that I hadn't stepped on the bird at all. And that I had been strong enough to clean up my own mess. But Amy knew what I wanted even before I did. She knew I wanted it dealt with, and she did it for me.

"It's OK, Bits," she says, resting her hand on my arm. "It was an accident. It isn't your fault." And I know she wants to put it behind us, to go into the Revelry glowing. Because we've made it. I can hear voices now too, and music.

But all of my excitement has evaporated away, leaving only a sticky residue of apprehension. Which isn't how I want to go into the Revelry.

There is no turning back now. There is only me, and Amy, and the Revelry.

So I take a deep breath and take a shaky step forward. Watching where I step this time.

"Let's go," I say. She grabs my hand, and squeezes three times: one long, two short. A variation on the handshake we used to do when we were little. I squeeze her hand back, suddenly filled with confidence that we'll be fine. Because we're together. And we have our rings, so we won't lose each other.

We follow the distant sounds of the lake lapping against the shore. There's something else too, a song that winds and twists its way towards us. An eerie, pale light grows brighter and brighter the closer we get. It shifts in the trees, and shadows move inside it. Mixed in with the damp smell of the woods, and the fresh smell of the eucalyptus, is a faint tang of smoke. And I realize I don't know what we'll find at the lake shore, what we'll find at the Revelry.

Amy squeezes my hand again. Just once this time. "This is going to be the best night of our lives," she whispers, eyes alight. "I can feel it."

four

I wake up gasping.

I'm not in the woods. *But where am I?*

I look around, blinking in the dim light. My head is spinning and my feet hurt, and there's a sharp pain in my finger.

The air smells like apples.

Apples... I'm in my family's orchard shed, where the apple presses are. That means I'm home, or close to it.

My hair is damp and I'm wrapped in a tartan blanket. Underneath, my toga is damp and singed at the edges, and it reeks of smoke.

And I'm alone.

"Amy?" I croak, my throat raw and sore. It must be morning. Birds chirp and warm light seeps in through the edges of the shed door. But where is Amy? Panic claws up my chest before my eye catches on a pile of rags in the corner.

I hobble over to the rags, my bare feet ache like I've been dancing all night, or maybe running, and my sandals are nowhere to be found, and, *oh*, it isn't Amy.

Just her toga. Or what's left of it. The material is damp and the edges singed just like mine. But I'm still in mine. And I'm here. And Amy is not. *Where is she?*

A sharp stab of pain shoots from my hand throughout my whole body, screaming for my attention. I look down and gasp.

Where my twisted ring should be, the delicate braid of hair that connects me to Amy, is a raised and ropey scar, encircling my finger. It's red and angry, and it hurts to touch.

What happened?

And most importantly, *where is Amy?*

I take a deep breath and the acrid smell of the burnt material mingles with the familiar sweet smell of pressed apples. The door to the shed creaks open and more light floods in.

And with it, Amy.

"There you are!" I say. My whole body sags in relief, like the strings of anxiety that had been holding me taut, like a marionette, relax.

Her hair is damp too, but unlike me, she's dressed – in *my* clothes. A pair of sweatpants and an old T-shirt. And she's holding two cups of steaming tea.

"Good morning, sleepy head," she says cheerfully, like all I've done is overslept after a house party dancing to bad music, or from staying up all night watching movies. Like I'm not wrapped in a blanket that isn't mine, with singed clothes on underneath. Like I didn't wake up in the orchard shed.

"What happened?" I demand. I don't remember *anything*. As this realization sinks in, a cold spreads through me and I begin to shiver. "Ames?"

"We went to the Revelry," she says simply. She hands me my tea and I take a tentative sip and stare back at her, racking my brain. What happened? What was the last thing I can remember? The woods, walking in the woods, stepping on the bird and then, in the distance, Lake Lost.

"Do *you* remember any of it?"

"I don't think we're meant to remember it," she says, her voice oddly dreamy.

"But … but!" I sputter. "Our togas! And this!" I brandish my index finger at her, where my ring scar is raised and red and angry. "What happened?" I look to her finger and gasp. She has a matching scar.

Well, almost matching. It is raised, like the hair ring

we made has somehow slipped beneath our skin, but where mine is red, like a welt, her ring is white.

"How do you explain that?" I grab her hand and hold it next to my own.

Amy glances down at her finger like she's just noticed the scar for the first time. And maybe she has. "Something must have happened," she says, her voice dreamy in a way that makes me shiver. Amy loves to talk about everything, to relive every experience again through stories; she will practically recreate a night complete with voices and impressions, but she doesn't want to talk about this?

"Yes, *something* happened and I want to know what! What was the point of going if we don't remember any of it?" My voice is shrill.

Amy shrugs, and her eyes glaze over a bit. "I remember music. There was dancing. I remember dancing." She begins to hum, and sway, and as she does the tune washes over me and I remember it too. But just barely, like a song I heard a long, long time ago.

But I know deep in my bones that I heard it last night.

"I'm scared something ... *bad* happened," I whisper.

"Like what?"

"Like ... someone did something to us. Something bad."

This pulls her out of her strange and dreamy state. She shakes her head vehemently.

"I know we were together the whole time. And I would never, ever let anything bad happen to you." She looks closely at me, for the first time that morning. "And how do you feel?"

I pause. My feet hurt, and there's the burn on my finger, but when I stretch beneath my ruined toga, nothing feels wrong. I don't feel violated in any way. I'm not sore and there is no bruising or tenderness anywhere, no cuts or scrapes on my skin. Just the burn on my finger.

"But our rings…" I hold out my finger again, where our promise not to lose each other has been burned into something else entirely on our skin. "This looks like something bad."

Amy stares down at both our hands. "Maybe it was the price we paid to go to the Revelry."

"And our burnt togas?"

"They were cheap sheets. Probably spontaneously combusted."

She laughs like she's said something funny. I stare back at her, mind whirling.

"Bits, come on," she says, sounding almost annoyed. "I was with you the whole night. I remember that. Don't you?"

And that rings true in my mind. Even though I can't wade through the murky memory of the night, I know I was with her.

Amy leans close to me, her eyes clear. "You're OK, Bitsy. We're both OK. We're home and we're safe."

Five

I don't care about getting in trouble for sneaking out.

I want to tell my parents what happened.

Or I want to tell them that I don't know what happened.

They went to their own Revelry, years ago. Maybe they can tell me more. Answer the questions I have.

I think about how to tell them, about what to tell them, as I stand in a scalding hot shower. My feet are filthy, and I watch as the dirt and grime wash off and disappear down the drain. Like it was never even there.

My hair is matted, and it takes a long time to shampoo. As I'm scrubbing at my scalp, I wince. Something hurts.

Gingerly I feel around the back of my head. There's a huge lump there. I don't know how I didn't notice it before.

At first panic claws up my throat. Do I have a concussion? Do I need to go to the hospital? But then a strange sense of relief floods through me.

That is why I can't remember what happened. I must have hit my head. And I'm fine now, aren't I? If I'd really hurt myself, I wouldn't have woken up.

The thought chills me, despite the heat of the water rushing over me. But at least that is one mystery solved.

I wonder if I should tell my parents about the bump on my head. But how to explain that I don't know how I got it? They'll understand, I tell myself when I get dressed and stare at my reflection in the mirror, trying to trigger a memory of what happened.

I am anxious about telling them. I've always been a rule follower. I come home when I say I will; I get good grades; I don't lie to my parents.

Until now. And sneaking into a Revelry that isn't my own isn't just breaking my parents' rules. It is breaking the unspoken rules of Ember Grove.

When they come home, I avoid them because I'm not ready to talk yet. I don't know how. I've never done this before. It feels strange, like I'm playing a part of the kid who has to confess to their parents. This isn't me – this isn't Bitsy Clark.

It weighs on me all day. And then finally, we all sit down for dinner. Me, my dad, and my mom. My dad has made cheesy chicken casserole with green chilis. One of my favourites, but I barely taste it as I chew. I can do this. I can tell them. I *have* to tell them.

"Something happened," I say, and then I start to cough. Not a small cough. A small piece of chewed-up chicken flies out of my mouth, and I still keep coughing. I'm coughing so hard I can't breathe. My throat burns.

My mom leaps into action, scooting out of her chair so fast it leaves a mark on the floor as she comes and whacks me on the back. "Bitsy! Take a deep breath, honey."

"She's all right, Laura," my dad says. "Sounds like something just went down the wrong pipe."

Finally the coughing subsides and I take in a long, shaky breath. My eyes are watery.

My mom sits back down in her chair and passes me my cup of water, which I take and gulp down gratefully.

I open my mouth to speak again, and my throat starts to tighten.

"Last night," I begin, and then the coughing starts again. It is only when I stop trying to talk, stop trying to tell them about the Revelry that the coughing subsides. But my throat still burns in warning.

My mom's gaze catches on my ring scar. "Oh, honey!

What happened here?" She takes my hand to examine it more closely and I'm so grateful – this is how she'll know something weird happened. Something I can't talk about. She turns my hand over in her own, focusing on my ring burn. It isn't as red and angry as it was this morning, but the skin is still puckered. "It looks like a burn."

"It is," I say, the words falling easily off my tongue. So I try again. "But I don't know how I got it." This is good! I keep going. "Last night…" And then my throat tightens again, and I stop before the coughing can start. I clear my throat. "Weird, huh?" I say.

"I'll get you some ointment," my mom says, releasing my hand.

I want her to keep holding it. I want to stay close to her, like I'm small again.

Later that night, I go over to my grandma's. Talking to her always makes me feel better.

She lives in the house next door, so I don't have to go far. My dad was born in that house, and as the family orchard business grew and boomed, it made sense for him to stay and join the business. I loved coming to visit her when I was little, and I still do. Her house always smells the same, like pine mixed with apple pie.

Through her front window, I can see the flickering

of the TV. I let myself in and wander into the living room. Sure enough, Grandma Shirley is sitting in front of the television, the sound blaring so loud I wince. She's in her favourite chair, a massive recliner covered in giant roses, with her feet up. It's a custom-made recliner that we bought for her a few years back, and she would live in it if she could. She's wearing her slippers with the pompoms on the toes, and what she calls her "evening attire", which is basically a fancy silk nightgown.

The Bachelor is on. Grandma Shirley loves reality TV and there's always plenty for her to watch.

"Hi, Grandma," I call out from the doorway. She looks up, and her eyes brighten. She mutes the TV, but doesn't turn it off.

"Bitsy! Come in, come in! Actually, could you get me a cup of tea? I've been hankering after one for the last two episodes but didn't have it in me to get up. I'm just so damn comfortable here."

I wonder for a moment if it is more than that, if she's having more trouble getting up and around these days. "Grandma Shirley," I say, "have you had dinner?"

She gives me a sheepish shake of her head. I sigh.

"I'll bring you tea, and then I'll make you something for dinner too. You should have come over tonight."

Grandma Shirley raises her brows. "And miss my shows?"

I laugh and head into the kitchen. I'm barely gone before I hear the TV blaring again. In the fridge, I find towers of Tupperware, all labelled and dated. My parents bring over meals once a week for her to easily heat up. My dad once said it was the best of all possible worlds: my grandma feels independent and my parents know that she has plenty to eat.

Of course that is making the assumption that she is getting out of her reality TV recliner and actually heating up the food.

I grab a Tupperware of mac and cheese and pop it in the microwave. While it heats up, I make a cup of tea the way Grandma Shirley likes it.

I carry everything in on a tray and prop it on her lap. She mutes the volume of the TV again, but doesn't turn it off. I'm not surprised or offended. I don't think she ever turns it off.

"Now tell me," she says between bites of mac and cheese, "what have I done to earn the honour of a visit from my favourite granddaughter?"

"I'm your only granddaughter," I say.

"How embarrassing it would be for you if you weren't my favourite then," she says with a wink.

"Do I need a reason to visit my grandma?"

"You tell me," she says.

"Grandma," I say slowly, anticipating the cough attack. "What do you remember about your Revelry?" The words get out. My throat doesn't burn.

Grandma Shirley turns towards me slowly, and then, to my enormous surprise, she turns off her TV.

"My Revelry?" she says. "Oh, that brings back memories. Must have been over sixty years now. When I think of my Revelry, I think of your grandpa."

My grandparents were high-school sweethearts. Just like my parents. Our Ember Grove roots go deep. But Grandma Shirley is the only grandma I've got left. My mom's parents died in a car accident when I was little — they moved here before she was born, but too late to have a Revelry of their own. Not like Grandma Shirley.

"I've not talked about my Revelry in a long time," she says in a dreamy voice. "One of the best nights of our life, our Revelry." Her eyes mist over. And part of me thinks I should stop asking about it. But another part of me, a bigger part, wants to know. *Needs* to know.

"But what happened?" I push. "What made it so special?"

"Why ... it was our Revelry," she says, but she's starting to frown. "It's more of a feeling I get than anything. It was a long time ago. But I know that the Revelry changed everything for us." She closes her eyes for a long moment and I think she's fallen asleep, but then she jolts up and grabs my hand in her own, holding tight. "The apples, the apples came later."

I smile back at her. "Yes, I know you and Grandpa bought the orchard in your twenties." This is Clark family lore. How my grandpa bought what everyone thought was a blighted plot of land and turned it into Clark Orchards, with the sweetest apples ever grown in Ember Grove. He sold them to grocery stores all over the country, and then when my dad joined the family business, he started making small-batch apple juice and apple cider and apple anything. "But can you tell me more about the actual Revelry? What do you remember about it?"

"You'll go to your own Revelry one day," says Grandma Shirley with a slightly dazed smile. My heart leaps into my throat. I've already had one. One that wasn't my own. One that I stole – only now I'm paying the price. "And your Revelry will change everything. It always does."

"But what *happens*?"

Her eyes drift over my shoulder and she begins to hum. The same song that Amy was humming this morning. The tune drifts inside my ears and burrows into my brain. I shake my head, trying to shake it off of me.

"Yes, Grandma?" I say loudly, louder than the tune she's humming. "What were you saying?"

Grandma Shirley blinks a few times, and then she rubs her temples. "Oh, Bitsy, I'm so sorry, I'm getting the most terrible headache. It's just come on out of nowhere. Here, let me put back on my show. That always distracts me from my headaches." She clicks the TV on and the room is filled with the sound of a man declaring his undying love to a woman he's just met. Grandma Shirley settles back into her chair, eyes bright again. "That one," she says, gesturing at the TV, "she is not in it for the right reasons."

"Grandma Shirley, I have to tell you something," I try again. But my mouth is dry and my throat is itchy, almost burning again, and the rest of the words won't come.

"Hush. I don't want to miss this part."

So I hush. And I sit and watch the rest of the episode with her, and then I wash and put away her dishes.

"Thank you, sweetheart," she says. "You're a good girl."

I wonder whether, if I died tomorrow, that is what they'd put on my tombstone. *Bitsy Clark: A Good Girl.*

Sometimes I want to be more than a good girl. I want to be brave. Or fascinating. But I don't say this to my grandma. I just lean over and kiss her on her cheek.

"Oh! That reminds me! You're starting at Chanterelle's this year, aren't you?"

50

A job at Chanterelle's is coveted in Ember Grove. Chanterelle's is a tea-house and organic shop at the edge of the woods, but on the far side of the woods from here, down near the cemetery. It's been around for years and is run by a woman who calls herself Chanterelle, like the mushroom. My mom worked there when she was in high school. And it has always been expected that I will too.

Rumour has it that Chanterelle will tell fortunes using the tea-leaves she sells, but only after hours, and only out the back. I've always wanted to ask her to tell my fortune, but I've always been a little bit afraid of Chanterelle. She's tall and thin, with limbs so long she looks like a stick insect with glasses. She's friends with my grandma and sometimes, when I come over here, the two of them are sitting, cackling and drinking their tea. The way Chanterelle looks at you makes it easy to believe that she really can tell your fortune. That she can tell everything you're thinking with one look.

Chanterelle always hires high-school students to work after school, and she's flexible on the hours, and the pay is great. Usually she hires seniors, but because she's friends with my grandma, this year she's hired me and Amy.

"We start next week." I lean in and give her a quick hug. "Thank you for that. For asking her to hire me and Amy. You are the best."

51

"If you think helping you get a job makes me the best, what about this?" she says, rummaging in the pocket of her silk robe. She pulls out a set of keys. "Thought you might want to drive to school this year. Drive to your new job too." Her eyes twinkle at me. "It's your junior year, isn't it? You'll need a car now. And you'll look fetching in the yellow."

"You're giving me your car!"

"I'm *lending* you my car," she corrects. Then she grins. "It isn't like I can take it out myself, can I? My licence has just expired and I have a feeling I wouldn't pass the driving test these days." She leans forward and waggles a finger at me. "My one condition is you have to drive me around wherever and whenever I wish!"

I pretend to ponder it. "What if you ask me to drive you across the country to New York City on a school night?"

Grandma Shirley gives an elaborate shrug. "Then you'll have to do it. A fair trade, I'd say."

"Hmm," I say. And then I can't hide my smile any longer. "You drive a hard bargain, but I'll take it."

I kiss her on her cheek. Her skin feels soft and paper thin.

Sometimes, being a good girl has its perks.

Six

I am determined to find out more. To find out what happened.

Amy won't talk to me about it. Her eyes glaze over and she gets bored.

"You're the one who has always been obsessed with the Revelry," I tell her when we are at the vintage shop in town, running our hands over old dresses with their own stories to tell and soft T-shirts with their memories as faded as the print. The owner of the shop, Ms Hamilton, is in the front, talking to another customer. I wonder whether if she was any closer, I'd have been able to ask Amy about the Revelry. If I'd even have been able to say the words out loud.

Amy sighs heavily. "I was obsessed with *going* to it. And then we did," she said. "That itch has been scratched."

"But ... but ... we don't know what happened!" I sputter.

"Maybe nobody knows what happens."

And then that song, the song that is haunting me, comes on over the speakers of the shop. Amy smiles and begins to sway in time with the music.

I even text my older brother, Harvey, about it. After all, he went to his own Revelry just a few years ago.

But my messages are never delivered. I can see them on my phone, but they never go through. When I text him about anything else, when he's coming home next, how things are at Cobalt, those go through fine. It's just these that sit with a little undelivered 'X' next to them.

So I try to email him instead – but any mention of the word Revelry gets the email bounced back.

I'm desperate enough to call him (and I *never* call him), but after five minutes, when I bring up the Revelry, the call drops.

When I tell Amy about this, she simply shrugs.

"Stranger things have happened in Ember Grove," she says, and I get a chill because that is what *I* tell *her* when weird things happen. This is the first time she's said it to me, like she is the one who belongs here, who can accept the unexplained, and I'm the one with the questions. The one who's an outsider.

And when I Google "Revelry Ember Grove" *nothing,* absolutely nothing comes up.

It is like it has never happened.

The only proof I have is my ring scar.

At least Amy and I came home, I tell myself. Not everyone makes it home from their Revelry.

It's the last night of summer vacation, school is starting tomorrow and Amy comes over so we can pick out what we want to wear on the first day back.

Maybe it's silly or juvenile to plan out what to wear with your best friend, but to me and Amy, it is tradition.

It started the night before the first day of fourth grade, after Amy and I had been inseparable all summer. She was at my house for dinner, like she often was (and often still is), and my mom realized Amy didn't have anything new to wear for the new school year. So she quietly drove to the mall in the next town over, and bought two matching dresses. One for me and one for Amy. We wore them on the first day of fifth grade, but the following year we didn't match because we thought we were too old and too cool, so we *coordinated*, and then every year after that neither of us could imagine getting ready for a new school year without picking our first-day outfits together.

As soon as we're in my room and my door is closed, I start talking about it.

"Ames, now I know why we could never find anything about the Revelry. There is nothing to find," I say. "Look what happens when I look it up." I thrust my phone under her nose.

Amy sighs and pushes my phone away, and begins to rummage through my closet.

"We already knew that," she says. "I don't know why you are so surprised. There has never been any information available about it to anyone. Why would that change this year? You need to let it go."

"But that doesn't explain why we can't remember anything," I say. "Unless you hit your head too? I mean, your toga was burned as badly as mine was."

Amy turns and fixes me with a look. "Bitsy! I don't want to talk about it any more. You are the one always telling me that the woods like to keep their secrets. *Let it go.*"

"You don't think it is weird that neither of us remembers anything?"

"I remember..." She starts to hum and runs her finger absently along her ring scar. That song again. My skin prickles. Why is that the only thing we can remember? And why doesn't Amy think it is a big deal?

Both of our scars have turned white, but I can still feel our twisted hair beneath my skin, like a small snake encircling my finger.

Then Amy shakes her head. "There's nothing to talk about. You know the rules better than me. Nobody talks about their Revelry."

"But *something* happened," I say. "I know it."

"Bitsy, we're fine. We're safe." Amy squeezes my hand. "Don't worry."

"OK," I say, even though I don't mean it. I think of Florence Lonsdale. The girl who never made it home from her Revelry. Who I want to look up online but am too scared to see what I'll find.

"Good." Amy's tone is definitive, like that is the end of it, and we'll never speak of it again. Like she doesn't have the chorus of *what happened what happened what happened?* playing on repeat in her brain. Maybe she doesn't. Maybe it's just me.

I flop back on my bed and stare out of my window. We never should have gone. But there's no point in trying to talk about it any more. To anyone. I should listen to Amy. I should just let it go.

What happened what happened what happened? chants the voice in my head.

Nothing. But that feels wrong. That feels like a lie.

I *have* to know.

But not tonight. Tonight I will think about what I'm going to wear to school tomorrow. In the morning I'll pick Amy up and we'll go into the new year side by side, ready to take on anything.

"Oh, I like this." Amy pulls out a long silk skirt.

"Way too fancy for school," I say, getting up to put it back.

As I hang up the silk skirt, my hand grazes on something soft. It's a cream cashmere sweater my grandma gave me for Christmas. Grandma Shirley has excellent – and expensive – taste. I haven't worn it yet. I've been saving it.

Amy's eyes light up. "I love that!" she says, grabbing it. "Can I try it on?"

She takes off her own shirt and pulls on the sweater without waiting for a response. It looks amazing on her. Better than it looks on me.

I push down my rising envy. Amy and I always share clothes. This is nothing new. "It looks great on you," I say. She scrutinizes herself in the mirror, piling her purple hair on top of her head, then letting it fall.

Amy looks good in everything. Her confidence magically morphs every article of clothing to suit her body perfectly.

She catches my eye in the reflection. "You should wear it," she says, quickly stripping it off and holding it out to me.

The sweater hangs between us. In that moment, I want to wear it. If only because if I do, then Amy can't.

Be a good friend, Bitsy. I take a breath and shake my head adamantly. "Honestly, it looks amazing on you."

Part of me wants her to argue, to say it looks better on me, that I should wear it. But then she pulls the sweater back over her head. "Only if you are sure," she says, her voice muffled from behind the cashmere.

"I'm sure," I lie.

She pops her head out and grins at me. "You're the best."

We sift through my closet together, holding up various options, each shirt or dress a memory in itself.

Amy unearths a black knitted dress with a V-neck tucked in the back of my closet that I don't remember ever wearing before, or even buying. That's weird. Maybe my mom bought it for me. But something about it doesn't sit well with me. I know what is in my closet. And I've never seen this before.

"This is it," Amy says, tossing it to me. "Put it on." The dress is snug on me, and a little short – maybe my mom bought it for me a few years ago – but Amy *oohs* and *ahs*. "You look hot." Then she studies me. "Maybe pin your

59

hair back like this," she says, pushing a clip into my hair. "There!" She beams. "Now we both have amazing looks for tomorrow."

I know Amy would have given me the cream sweater if I'd really wanted it, but this way I get to be the magnanimous one. I'm as snug in the feeling of being generous as I am in the black dress. For a moment, I don't think about the Revelry at all.

Seven

Whenever Amy and I say goodbye, it always feels like an ellipsis … like we're just pausing our conversation before we can pick back up again.

But ever since the Revelry, something feels off. We've never had things we don't talk about.

I usually tell Amy everything. From random dreams I have, to my childhood crush on Jonah who works at the deli (I think I confused my love of sandwiches with love for the teenage boy who made me said sandwiches). And Amy tells me everything too. We even talk about Amy's dad, and I know I'm the only person Amy will confide in about him. After Amy's mom died when she was little, her dad became obsessed with gambling. Changing the family's luck, he claimed. He wasn't too terrible at it, but he wasn't great either, doing well enough to support himself, but not himself *and* a kid. So he asked Aunt Lily to take Amy in. Her dad is still trying to become a pro poker player, or something. He used to visit more, but he hasn't been to Ember Grove in years. There isn't anything to say about him now, but I know Amy would talk to me about him if she needed to. But now all I want to talk about is the Revelry.

And I can't.

Maybe Amy's right. I need to put it out of my head.

I drive her home, the first time we've driven in Grandma Shirley's yellow car, and we make plans for the next morning. For what time I'll pick her up to drive her to school. Just as we've always walked to school together, even though it was out of my way, now we'll drive together.

By the time I'm back at my house, the setting sun is turning the sky pink and gold, and I want to watch it set. There's a tree in the orchard that I think of as *my* tree. It has been my favourite one to climb since I can remember. I make my way through the orchard until I find it. As I haul myself up, I start to hum absent-mindedly. Hand over hand, going higher in the tree so I can have a better view of the sunset. Suddenly, I realize what song I'm humming. That it's the song. The Revelry song. I cut off mid-note, trying to ignore the shiver running down my spine.

In the sudden quiet, another voice picks up the tune. Whistling it now, not humming. I grip on to the tree, palms sweaty, and stare through the leaves, trying to see where the sound is coming from. I almost expect the trees themselves to be whistling.

There's someone in the orchard with me. The first thing I notice is her hair. It's long, past her waist, and so blonde it looks almost silver. She's leaning against a big Crimson Crisp tree, directly across from me, with the apples hanging around her like jewels.

And she's watching me. *Waiting* for me. She looks satisfied and dangerous, like a fox that has snuck into a chicken coop.

I wonder if that makes me the chicken.

As she looks up and pins me with her gaze, I nearly fall out of the tree.

I've seen her before.

A memory crashes into me.

She was at the Revelry.

Lake Lost, glistening in the moonlight like a sheet of black glass.

And the revellers, all in togas, swaying gently in the wind like plants sprouting out of the sand.

All silent. Until the drums begin to pound, forcing my heart to beat in time with them.

And a masked girl with long, blonde hair, so light it glows silver in the night, and piercing grey eyes, climbing atop a plinth.

"Welcome!" she shouts. "Welcome to the Revelry!" A firecracker sets the sky alight. More music, with a low bass I feel in my bones.

Then I'm spinning with Amy and we're laughing and then a stranger is twirling me and I'm so swept up in it all I barely notice who I'm dancing with, just that I'm dancing, dancing, dancing, and then I'm back with Amy. Both breathless and starry eyed.

We are transformed. No longer teenagers wrapped up in sheets playing pretend. We're not just witnessing something spectacular. We are something spectacular.

The dancing goes on and on. And overseeing it all is the girl in the silver mask with silver hair.

She's here. The girl from the Revelry. She's here right in front of me. Proof that it happened, proof that I was there. She may be unmasked but I would recognize her anywhere.

"You!" I breathe. "You were at…"

She raises her finger to her lips to silence me, and as she does I stop talking.

Did I stop talking on my own or did she stop my words?

She glances over her shoulder. At my house, where I can hear my dad calling for me.

"Not here. Not now," she says. Her voice slides over me like silk. "Midnight. Meet me at the edge of the woods. At the bottom of this orchard."

Her words hang in the air like a dare. Midnight. It echoes what Amy had said the night of the Revelry.

I know better than to go into the woods at night with someone I don't know.

And yet… I want answers. I want proof. And here it is, standing right in front of me in the form of a silver-haired girl.

She smiles, looking more fox-like by the second, before she disappears into the orchard, leaving me alone in the tree, with nothing but that song running through my head.

I know that I'm going to sneak out to see her.

I have to.

The rest of the evening passes in a blur. All I can think about is that tonight I'm finally getting answers. I'm finally going to know what happened.

The silver-haired girl is waiting for me, half shrouded in darkness.

"You came," she said, her voice low and silky. She's barefoot and wearing black jeans and a sleeveless green top. She looks effortlessly glamorous, comfortable in her own skin in a way I never feel. If I'd thought about it, I would have worn something nicer than an oversized sweatshirt and ratty leggings.

We stare at each other for a beat, like we're in a competition to see who can hold the other's gaze the longest.

I look away first. Over her shoulder. Into the woods.

I know these woods. I grew up running around in them, playing hide-and-seek and tag, building forts.

I'm a girl from Ember Grove. These are my woods. Before and after the Revelry, the woods are mine.

I don't fear these woods.

And I don't fear this girl.

I step towards her, and she doesn't move, doesn't stir. Her body is all coiled, thrumming energy, like a cat about to pounce. I step around her and take two steps further into the woods. "Coming?" I say over my shoulder.

She nods, her pale eyes unreadable.

And we step into the darkness.

Eight

The moon is high and bright and its light filters down through the leaves. I lead, stepping confidently through the trees, knowing without having to look where there are raised roots and where the ground slopes suddenly. Until I remember the bird I crushed, when the woods I know, my woods, turned on me.

This slows me down, makes me watch the trees more carefully. A breeze rustles my hair and the air smells like earth and dirt and something strangely sweet. I wonder if we'll end up at Lake Lost.

I wonder if I've made a mistake coming back to the woods so soon.

The path opens up suddenly, and unexpectedly, into a clearing that I don't remember ever seeing. Only it's not just a clearing.

There's a living room in the woods.

I stand at the edge of the clearing, not daring to go closer.

A couch, overgrown with moss that looks both soft and slick to the touch; a warped and worn coffee table that looks like it has sprouted from the earth itself; an oversized armchair, vine tendrils crawling up the side. I blink, expecting it to disappear, but it all stays there.

"This is delightful," the girl says, and I jump. She's closer than I thought she was.

In all my years of running wild in the woods of Ember Grove, I've never seen this. And it doesn't look like something that could have sprung up overnight.

This is strange, even for Ember Grove.

Even for the woods.

My companion saunters forward, arms out like she owns the place. Then she looks up at me and laughs. "You should see your expression. Relax."

"You must not be from around here," I reply. Although of course she must, because how else would she have been at the Revelry? "Or you would know better than to just 'relax' in the middle of the woods."

"Here's what I know about *our* woods," she says. The way she says *our* makes my skin prickle. "Sometimes they give, sometimes they take, and this..." she spins around a bit. "This is a gift." She flops down on the couch, legs up on the coffee table. "And what is that saying about gifts? And horses?"

"Don't look a gift horse in the mouth," I say.

"Exactly."

"I don't know if that applies here," I say.

She laughs. "Worried that the three bears might come home and see that you've climbed in their bed, Goldilocks?"

I flush, embarrassed that she thinks I'm young and afraid. With all the confidence I can muster, I settle into the armchair. Something sharp pokes my spine but I ignore it and lean back. If she's comfortable here, so am I.

I take a moment to study her, grateful that the moonlight is bright enough that I can see her clearly. She has one of those faces that appears ageless. Like she's been carved from stone. A face you could imagine as easily on a medieval queen, or on an astronaut commander landing on a new planet.

A face impossible to forget. Those slate-grey eyes, a small upturned nose, sharp cheekbones. And that silvery hair that falls past her waist.

My own hair is tangled and in need of a wash, piled on top of my head in a sloppy bun.

"A bold move, going to a Revelry that wasn't your own," she says, one eyebrow quirking up as she flicks a strand of hair out of her face. I notice her long nails, how sharp they are. My own are bitten down to the quick and I ball my hands into fists to hide them.

"It is just a stupid party," I say. But I'm trembling.

She gives me a hint of a smile, like she's letting me in on a joke.

"You don't believe that, do you?" Then she tilts her head to the side. "You and your friend – the one with the violet hair – so loyal to each other. It's potent stuff, that kind of loyalty. The woods drink it up. And they'll want more of it too."

"You aren't making any sense," I say, trying to keep my voice light.

"It wasn't your Revelry," she says again. "And as the Revelry Master, well, it was my job to make sure the woods know we take it seriously." This time her smile is feral and makes the hair stand up on the back of my neck. "I couldn't have asked for a better result."

Revelry Master? What the hell is that? But I realize she *remembers*. More than that: she was in charge.

"What happened?" I say, leaning forward.

In response, she reaches into her back pocket and pulls out a box of matches. Keeping her eyes on mine, she lights a match and lets it burn all the way down. Until it's about to burn her fingers.

"Careful!" I cry, leaping out of the armchair and blowing the match out.

She leans back into the chair and laughs, still holding the blackened matchstick. She waves it back and forth in front of me, the way a cobra dances. The smell of the match makes my head swim. I blink and flames flare up behind my eyelids.

"I don't know why you're kicking up such a fuss," she says, still watching me. "You're both fine, aren't you? Saved by each other. It's poetic, really." The feral smile spreads. "But who knows what the woods will ask for now."

"The woods don't ask for anything. And the party is over." I try to keep my voice nonchalant, but *saved by each other* echoes in my ears. What is she talking about?

"You're a girl from Ember Grove, aren't you? You know these woods. You must know that sometimes they take." She winks. "Besides, the Revelry is never really over." And then she strikes fast as a snake, grabbing my hand and turning it over so it is palm up.

I'm so stunned I don't move.

Her own hands are rough. She runs her thumb over my ring scar. "Nifty souvenir."

I snatch my hand back. "This isn't funny," I say, glaring at her as I sit back in the armchair. I can feel my frustration waking up like a living thing inside of me.

71

She smirks. "It's a little funny."

"Why did you come and find me? In my orchard? I thought you were going to tell me what happened." Instead she's playing games with me, laughing at me.

She arches a brow. "I never said anything of the sort. All I told you was to meet me at the edge of the woods. And you did. I must say, I'm impressed. I wasn't expecting you to show. Even after I saw your spectacular bravery at the Revelry. I'll admit, I was curious about the girl who broke Revelry rules." She pauses and leans forward, eyes bright. "I was curious about *you*, Bitsy Clark."

I shudder. The way she says my name sounds like she's casting a spell. I feel like I'm not in my life, like I'm acting out a scene in a movie or in a dream, like nothing I do or say will come back to haunt me in the morning.

Or maybe it all will.

"You aren't the first Clark to go to a Revelry," she goes on.

"Everyone knows my family has been going to Revelries for years."

"And yet you still know so little about what goes on. No family secrets have been passed down to you, no warnings whispered." Her smile flashes again, and her voice turns patronizing. "Did you think that if you went to a Revelry you'd find out everything you'd always wanted to know?"

Despite everything, I laugh a little. "I thought if I snuck out to a Revelry, I'd have the night of my life. That's what is promised to us. What gets whispered."

"Maybe you did?" The girl gives me a smug smile.

"Why did you seek *me* out after the Revelry? Why come to my orchard. Why not…?" I trail off, not wanting to say Amy's name. I'm anxious enough that she knows my name, especially because I don't know hers.

"Your friend? Fair question, as both of you broke the rules, showed stupidity and bravery in equal measure. But she wouldn't have known what she was doing, not really. She's not from here, is she? And she sleeps soundly in her little room, never wondering if the wind in the hall is really that at all. Not like you. You know to throw a penny in the fountain. You know to listen to the wind."

A chill passes over me as I realize that she knows where Amy lives, knows where she sleeps. And more than that, she knows my very thoughts.

Then the silver-haired girl laughs like windchimes. "Oh, Bitsy, your face shows your every thought. Don't be so shocked. I make it my business to know everything about my Revelry guests. Even the unexpected ones. And your friend is nothing like you, Bitsy. *You* are a girl raised on Revelry tales. You are a Clark. The Revelry runs in your very blood. You are a girl from Ember Grove. Your

73

friend may not have known what you two were getting into when you went to a Revelry that wasn't your own, but you did. Deep in your bones you knew, and still went." She laughs again. "I can't decide if that makes you terribly brave or terribly foolish."

"Probably both," I mutter. But strangely, and stupidly, I'm flattered. This mysterious person wanted to talk to *me*. Almost everyone I know would rather talk to Amy. She's the confident one, the interesting one, the one who can make a whole room laugh or a single person feel special. And sure, her glow rubs off on me, the way the sun does with the moon, but nobody has ever treated me like I give off my own light.

Until now.

"I would know you if you went to Ember High," I say. I would remember her, this silver-haired girl with eyes like a broken mirror.

"I'm not an Ember High senior. You could say I was home-schooled. But that doesn't mean I don't get a Revelry. Revelry rules still apply. After all, it has been going on long before Ember High even existed. The traditions of Ember Grove go back before any bricks and mortar. Only the trees themselves know when the Revelries began."

"Aren't you the Revelry expert," I mutter.

"You have no idea," she says, and her windchime laugh echoes in the air. But this time it sticks in my brain, like that song I can't forget.

Then a memory overtakes me.

Amy and I, wandering away from the lake. Laughing, stumbling on our feet from all the dancing. The edge of my toga snagging on a thorn. Finding a tree with the perfect spot for us to rest, like someone had carved it out with a spoon. Listening to the sounds of the Revelry. The laughter and the music. Thinking, Amy's right — nothing bad is going to happen.

Amy yawning. "I'm going to close my eyes, for just a second."

Her head resting on my shoulder. Me smiling to myself at the fact that Amy can always fall asleep at anytime, anywhere.

And then a new voice in the dark. "Well, well, well."

I look around, but I don't see anybody.

And then. Through the trees. Silver eyes watching us.

A shiver spider-walking up my back.

"We're just resting," I say, feeling like I need to

explain myself. Explain why we've taken a moment to step away from the Revelry.

"Let your friend rest. She'll need her strength."

Spider chills spreading.

"For what?"

A laugh like windchimes. "I can't tell you that. That would ruin the fun."

A horn blaring through the woods. A summons. Amy jerks her head up. "Did I miss anything?"

A pale hand in the dark, lifted to lips. An order to stay quiet.

"No," I say. And then, still watching the eyes in the dark. "I think we should leave now." While we still can, I think.

Amy, defiant. "I want to stay."

She knows I would never leave her.

Eyes in the dark twinkling in delight, because they know that too. Eyes watching us like we're rabbits caught in a trap.

Eyes that look like shattered, silvered glass.

I snap back to the moment I'm in and stare at the silver-haired girl across from me. The one with eyes like broken mirrors.

"You were in the woods, when Amy and I were resting. You told me she would need her strength…"

"See, you do remember some of it." She stretches back out on the mossy couch and puts her arms behind her head, crosses her ankles.

"I think I hit my head that night," I say slowly. "Did you see?"

She shrugs. "So much happened that night, it is hard to remember it all. Maybe you did? It doesn't matter, really."

"It matters to me! I want to know!"

"All you need to know is this, Bitsy Clark."

She looks me straight in the eye. "The woods never play fair."

Nine

I stay in the woods with the silver-haired girl until almost dawn. And I still don't know much more than I did before I met up with her. Not even her name.

She never confirms whether I really hit my head or not.

But, despite her not giving me any of the answers I'd been looking for, I feel drawn to her. I don't want to leave. I want to know more. More about the Revelry. More about this girl. Her confidence, her mysteriousness, her aloofness … it captivates me. Not in a romantic way – it feels more powerful than that. I come out of the woods wanting to be her.

I don't realize just how late I stayed out until I sleep through my alarm the next morning, and wake to four missed calls from Amy.

I rush to get ready, yanking a brush through my hair, dabbing concealer under my puffy eyes, curling my lashes, trying to hide my fatigue. It doesn't work.

By the time I'm outside the old hospital, Amy is already waiting for me, looking irritated. I've barely pulled to a stop before she flings the door open.

"Sorry!" I say quickly, even though I've already messaged that about six times.

"It's fine," she says, but she's clearly in a huff.

She yanks down the sun visor above the front seat and reapplies her red lipstick. Her hair is pulled to the side in a complicated braid.

If I'd picked her up early enough, I'd have asked her to do my hair too. As it is, my hair feels somehow both fluffy and flat. I run a hand through it, and it snags on a tangle.

"You look nice," I say, trying to thaw the icy tension building in the car. "The sweater really suits you." *My* sweater, I want to remind her.

"Thanks," she says flatly.

I sigh loudly. I'll admit, it's a little dramatic, but it isn't like I meant to be late. "Amy, I've already said I'm sorry. Let's not fight."

"Well, you shouldn't have been late then," she snaps.

"But it wasn't my fault!"

Amy throws her hands up in the air in frustration.

79

"Who else's fault could it be then?" She raises an eyebrow.

I press my lips together tightly.

I don't want to tell her about going into the woods to meet someone from the Revelry. I know she'll think it's weird, how obsessed I am with trying to figure out what happened that night, when she can accept it so easily. But it is more than that. If I tell her about the silver-haired girl, she'll want to meet her, and...

Everyone always wants to talk to Amy when they meet her. I don't resent Amy for that – it's one of the things I love about her. One of the things that makes me so glad she's my best friend.

But.

I like that the silver-haired girl wanted to talk to me.

"*I was curious about you, Bitsy Clark,*" she'd said. And I want to keep it that way. At least for a little longer.

"I just couldn't sleep," I say finally. "Weird dreams." And then. "I've been having weird dreams since we went to the Revelry." I'm not lying, I realize. I *have* been having weird dreams.

I settle into the satisfaction of not being *completely* untruthful with my best friend.

Amy nods. "I have too," she admits.

Then a strange thing happens: sound stops. I don't mean Amy goes quiet. I mean *everything*. I can't hear the hum of the car, or the wheels rumbling on the road beneath us, or anything. I look over at Amy, and her mouth is moving, and she's gesticulating, and I shake my head, like I'm shaking water out of my ears, and then suddenly the sound comes rushing back in.

"Weird, right?" she says.

I want to ask her if her world just went quiet too, but the trees along the narrow road are leaning closer and closer, like they want to hear what I'm going to say. One branch even scrapes my window. Almost like a warning. And then Amy sighs. "Anyway, I'm sorry for being so cranky about you being late."

I want to grab her peace offering with both hands and hold it tight to my heart. "No, *I'm* sorry. I should have been on time."

And I swear the trees straighten up, bored by our mundane almost-argument.

"I mean, you are doing me a favour by picking me up," she says with a grin. "I guess I could be a little more gracious about it."

I grin back, and the atmosphere in the car returns to normal.

Almost normal. Because the not-quite-truth that I've told her buzzes in the air – small, like a gnat, but there all the same.

We pull into the parking lot with minutes to spare.

"There's a spot over there. Next to Cecily and the girls," says Amy, pointing.

That's how it has been for the past few years. Me and Amy as a package deal, and then Cecily and the girls. The girls seem to rotate, Cecily choosing and changing her consort throughout the year. Once upon a time we were Cecily, Amy and Bitsy. We called ourselves the CAB Club. But then when we got to high school, things changed. Amy joined the Drama Club and auditioned for every show she could, I made the swim team and spent almost every morning before school in the pool, and Cecily started partying.

But even she knew better than to sneak into a Revelry.

We might not be the CAB Club any more, but there is no bad blood between us. Cecily invites us to the parties she throws, and she'll go to the opening night of whatever play Amy is in, and always wishes me good luck when she knows I've got a swim meet.

"Who's with her?" I ask.

"Tanya and Danielle." And then Amy sits up a little straighter, checks her lipstick in the mirror.

"Anyone *else* over there?" I say, grinning.

"Steve Fawcett."

"And who else?" I know who she's eying, but I want to make her squirm.

"And Mark Lee." She sighs. "Maybe this year he'll notice me."

Amy has had a crush on Mark Lee since we were twelve. She shamelessly flirts with him all the time, so you'd think he might have picked up on it (then again, she shamelessly flirts with everyone). I don't blame her for liking him. Mark is the kind of guy who has a genuine smile, who will ask how you are and actually listen, and remember. Plus, his parents own Lee's Bakery so he smells like fresh-baked bread, in a weirdly sexy way. He's confident enough not to have to do the whole "bro" thing with other guys – he knows he doesn't have to.

Plus he's absurdly attractive. He's tall and has black hair that swoops to the side, and this wide smile that makes his dark eyes crinkle up in the corners.

If it sounds like I have a crush on Mark Lee, well, he has that effect on everyone. When you talk to him, in that moment, you do have a crush on him.

But for me, it's not a crush that's stuck. Who knows, maybe if Amy hadn't staked her claim on him so many years ago, I might have allowed mine to develop. But as it is, I like him as a human and I like him for Amy. They seem like they would be the perfect fit, but for whatever reason, it hasn't happened yet.

"Everyone notices you, Ames." I roll my eyes, but I'm smiling.

"You know what I mean. *Notice* me, notice me. The way I notice him." She sighs again, more theatrically this time. Then she grins. "And Steve will notice you and we'll all double date and it will be magical."

Steve is Mark's best friend. He's basically a walking, talking action figure. Maybe there is more to him than there seems – most people have layers and depth, right? Although I suspect he is more of a turnip than an onion. Bland all the way through.

"Maybe," I say out loud, laughing a little. What I mean is: never.

Then I focus on trying to park. The spot next to Cecily is tiny, and I'm terrible at parking. I ask Amy to get out to help guide me in, but as she gets out of the car, Mark Lee saunters over.

"Hey, Amy," he says, with his wide Mark Lee smile. It isn't even directed at me, but I'm caught in the edge of his glow, and I can't help but feel a little flustered. "How've you been?"

Amy grins at him. "I'm good."

I'm watching this all happen through a rolled-down

window like some sort of creep. I cough, trying to get Amy's attention so she'll help me park. But if she hears, she ignores me.

"Well, you look good." Mark gives her a quick once-over and I expect Amy to say something snarky in reply, but instead she blushes and kind of giggles and I am agog. That is so not Amy's style. Mark nods towards Amy's sweater. *My* sweater. Must be a lucky sweater. "I like this," he says. "It looks soft."

"It is." Amy's voice is raspy and sultry at the same time. Jesus. I feel like I'm watching the opening to an erotic film. I cough again.

They both ignore me and then the bell rings. Now we're all going to be late. Especially me.

I swear. Loudly.

Still nothing from them.

So I lean on the horn.

That gets their attention. Amy jumps and Mark swivels his head towards me so fast he looks like a bobblehead doll.

"Hey, Clark." Mark smiles at me. I can't help but notice it isn't the same wattage as the smile he gave Amy. "Good to see you."

"Yeah, you too," I say. Then I look at Amy. "Can you help me park?"

"Oh, Bits, I've got Chemistry on the other side of campus. I gotta go now or I'll be late."

"No way," says Mark. "I've got Chem too. Mr Peterson?"

"Yes!"

"There's only one Chem teacher at Ember High," I say deadpan, but they aren't listening to me. Not only that, but they are walking away. Amy's laughing – her real laugh, the one she is sometimes self-conscious about because it kind of sounds like a goose honking, but it doesn't seem to be bothering Mark because he's laughing too, and brushing his hand against her shoulder. Probably commenting on how soft the sweater is. Of course it is soft. It's cashmere. Not that Amy knew that when she picked it out of my closet. And I wasn't going to make a big deal out of it and tell her it was too expensive for her to wear. But now, now I wish I was the one wearing it. I look down at this old black sweater dress that's already fraying at the edges. I felt nice in it last night when I tried it on, but in the light of day, here at school, it doesn't feel right.

I contemplate leaning on the horn again, but I don't want to ruin this for Amy. Anyway, what would I do? Demand that she stays to help me park?

"Fine," I mutter under my breath. "I'll do it myself."

By the time I've managed to park and made my way to English, I'm almost fifteen minutes late. The door creaks loudly as I push it open. Everyone whips their head around to stare at me, including my new English teacher, Ms Stuart.

"Sorry I'm late," I say, feeling my cheeks flame as I step inside the classroom.

Ms Stuart frowns at me. "Name?" she says. I haven't even sat down yet. I hover at the front of the classroom.

"Bitsy," I say. "Bitsy Clark."

"Not a very good first impression, is it, Miss Clark?"

"Sorry," I say again, ducking my head down. I feel more embarrassed than I should. I hurry to an empty desk in the middle of the class. There's a low rumble of laughter, which feels unnecessary. All I've done is walk in late.

"Miss Clark!" says Ms Stuart, even sharper now. I pause in the middle of the rows of desks. It's a tight squeeze. I feel like I'm practically on the laps of the students on either side of me. "Your dress, Miss Clark. That isn't suitable for the dress code."

"What?" I say, flabbergasted. Sure it's a bit snug, and a little short, especially since I'm so tall, but it's a knitted sweater dress. Nothing *that* scandalous. I glance down, trying to see where she could be finding fault and gasp.

The dress has unravelled. It must have snagged on the door, because I've left a trail of wool in my wake, unspooled behind me.

My ass is fully hanging out. My green underwear on display. Why the hell did I wear green underwear? Like bright green. Oh, I know why: *because I wasn't expecting to have it on display to my entire English class.* At least it isn't a thong. But, oh God, this is awful.

I try to pull what is left of the sweater dress down over my hips, but all that does is make it worse, the fabric unravels in my hands.

This feels almost … familiar. And suddenly a Revelry memory engulfs me, like a wave pulling me under the sea.

My toga snagging on something. A branch? A rock? Chanting all around me. And then heat, so much heat – not just heat, flames.

The smell of smoke.

My toga on fire.

On fire.

Me, desperately trying to get it off. And then so much smoke.

"I said *Miss Clark!*" Ms Stuart's voice is stern. I snap out of it and stare up at her. "Do you need to excuse yourself?"

I run out of the classroom, ignoring the laughter and catcalls behind me, unspooling like the yarn from my dress.

What is happening?

I burst into the bathroom, out of breath and my chest heaving. My reflection shows a blotchy red face. But the red patches spread down my neck too, and beneath the snug fit of the dress.

The dress has unravelled all the way up to the waistband of my underwear. But on top it feels unbearably tight, and I'm itchy underneath. So itchy.

I try to pull what remains of the dress over my head but it is somehow getting tighter and tighter by the moment and my arms can't get out of it and I'm so itchy oh my God I just want it off get it off get it off get it off...

I claw at the thread at the bottom, now wanting it to unravel, needing it to unravel, I need to get out of it, my skin feels like it is blistering underneath the fabric—

"Bitsy?"

I whirl around, covered in angry red hives, with fistfuls of wool in my hands.

It's Amy.

"Bitsy, what's going on?" she says, coming close. "What happened to your dress? And your skin, we have to get you to the nurse!"

"I … I can't let anyone see me like this!" My voice catches. The fabric is still tightening around my chest. I feel like I can't breathe.

With a grunt, I rip what is remaining of the dress off. My skin is covered in raised red hives. The only sound is my laboured breathing.

I go towards Amy, wanting a hug, but she leans back, away from me. Her eyes are wide, and for a moment, disgust flashes across her features. Like whatever I've got is catching.

"I'll get you my coat," she says quickly. "I'll be right back. In the meantime –" she grabs a handful of paper towels and runs them under the sink – "put these on your hives. It should help."

By the time Amy returns with her coat, my hives have almost disappeared. I'm waiting for her in one of the cubicles. I don't want to risk anyone seeing me with no clothes on and covered in a rash. I'm mortified and confused about what the hell happened and feel like I could burst into tears.

"You should go home," Amy says now, gently guiding my arms into the sleeves of her coat. She's being so kind

I wonder if I imagined her leaning away from me. That isn't like Amy. I must have mistaken her expression.

"Amy, my dress unravelled itself," I say, trying to get my head around what happened. "And then, it got so tight. It was like it was trying to strangle me."

"It's an old dress, Bits," says Amy pragmatically. "The fabric got caught. These things happen. You remember when my favourite pair of jeans split at the seams?"

"Your jeans split because you jumped into the splits while wearing them. This is not the same thing at all! And how do you explain my dress trying to strangle me?"

"You panicked. That's why your chest felt tight. And you must have had a bad reaction to the wool."

"That's not what happened!" I say. Something else occurs to me. "How did you know to come to the bathroom? To find me?" As close as Amy and I are, it isn't like she can read my mind. Something strange is happening, I know it.

An odd look crosses Amy's face. "It's so weird," she says. "I was sitting in Chem, and Mark asked me if I wanted to be lab buddies, which by the way is maybe the best thing that has ever happened to me." I raise my eyebrows. "Sorry, not the time, but then…" she trails off and holds her hand out to me.

The scar on her finger, the ring scar, is raised like a welt. Mine is the same.

"I felt like I had to come find you. I don't even remember how I ended up in this specific bathroom. It is on the other side of campus from where I was." She shakes her head and laughs a little. "Weird, right?"

"Yes," I say emphatically. "It is. Weird things are happening. Why aren't you freaking out?"

"Bitsy, it must be, like, our best-friend telepathy or something." Then she gives me a small smile. "Stranger things have happened in Ember Grove."

I groan. "I wish I had never taught you that phrase."

"Bitsy, you had an allergic reaction. You must have been itching without realizing it. Just a bit of bad luck. That's all."

I want to say more, I want to tell Amy about the memory I had, of the toga on fire, but first period will soon be finished and between classes the bathroom will be crowded and I don't want anyone to see me like this.

Amy walks with me to my car. I've got a pair of sweatpants in the back, and my swimsuit, but that's it. I'm going to have to go home to get a change of clothes.

"You can go," I say. "I'm fine."

I'm not, and she knows I'm not, but relief floods her face. "Great," she says. "Call me later, OK? Love you!" And then she walks away without looking back. In my sweater that fits her so perfectly. Confident, knowing she'll get the right kind of attention. Not the kind of attention that comes when you end up in your underwear in front of your entire English class. The worst part is, if our roles had been reversed, I know Amy would have pulled off having her dress unravel. She would have laughed about it, taken control of the situation, not let it take control of her.

Like how she is so calm about what happened at the Revelry. Like she conquered it merely by being there.

She isn't letting it haunt her. Not like it's haunting me.

Ten

I don't go back to school that day.

I call in, pretend to be my mom, and say I've had a severe allergic reaction.

Not entirely a lie.

I don't hear from Amy for the rest of the day. Not until right before bed, when she texts to see if I'm going to pick her up for school the next day. I fight the urge to ignore her message. I take a breath. I don't want to overreact. She hasn't done anything wrong.

It just doesn't feel like she's done anything right either.

The next day, she acts like everything is fine, everything is normal. She puts on our favourite songs and dances in the front seat to make me laugh, and I start to think maybe she's right – maybe it was just a freak coincidence that my dress unravelled and made me break out in a rash.

I tell myself this even as I see the trees overhead leaning in, like they did the day before, like they're listening to our conversations, like they want to see what is happening inside our car. I tell myself this even as the fog rolls in thick, thick, thick, even more than usual for Ember Grove. So thick that I have to turn on my headlights in the daytime.

I tell myself this lie even though I know there are no coincidences in Ember Grove.

At school, word spreads about my unravelling dress, and all week people tease me about it.

"Heard you put on quite a show," says Steve with a wink that I think he means to be charming but which comes off as creepy. It's during a break between classes, and we're in the parking lot.

I expect Amy to jump in and defend me, like she always does, but she's laughing at something Mark Lee has just said and isn't paying attention.

Cecily laughs, and it is a little meaner than I'd expect from her. "Bitsy, was your whole ass really out?"

I force a laugh too. "What a wardrobe malfunction." I'm trying to take control of this, the way I know Amy would. If I'm the one telling the joke, everyone is laughing with me, not at me.

95

I know all of my friends have seen me in a swimsuit and I change in front of people in the locker rooms, but there was something about it that felt so uncanny and strange. It wasn't just the dress falling apart, or the hives, it was all of it together. All I want is for people to forget about it. I try to think of something else to say, to change the topic, to distract everyone, but my mind goes blank. I need Amy, Amy who likes to be the star of the show and who can keep any conversation moving. But right now she's not paying any attention to me at all.

At least we've got Chanterelle's to look forward to.

We drive there after school, going down the dirt roads that skirt the woods, and park behind the cemetery.

The café is decorated like a woodland forest, which feels a little redundant since it's situated right at the edge of an actual forest. But this is woodland forest by way of Disney gone dark. The chairs are toadstools, the tables are tree trunks, and the floor underneath is thick and mossy, like actual grass. There is so much greenery on the walls it almost looks like they are breathing. The best table is right in the middle of the café, underneath a gigantic indoor weeping willow. To get to it you have to push through the hanging leaves and vines, and when you are underneath, it feels like you are completely alone. It feels a little on the nose for a woman named Chanterelle to not only open up an organic café and shop, but also to decorate it with mushrooms, but as they say, stranger things have happened in Ember Grove.

When I thanked Chanterelle for hiring us, she waved it off.

"I owed Shirley a favour," she said. I would have felt more guilty about the blatant nepotism, but it isn't like I was the only one benefitting from it. I was helping Amy out too. And I knew she needed the money. Aunt Lily doesn't give Amy much, and with this job she'll be able to buy things she wants and needs.

Today is our first official day working at the café. We had a training day over the summer that mostly consisted of Chanterelle showing us all her various herbs and mushrooms and other, stranger, ingredients that customers come here for. Then she showed us how to use the cash register. "We have a daily soup that I make in the morning and it stays warm on the hob all day, and I'm sure I don't need to show you how to make toast, tea or coffee. You don't look like idiots to me."

At the time I'd nodded, all confidence, but now it is my first day and I can't exactly remember where everything is.

"All right, ladies," says Chanterelle, sweeping onto the café floor. "I know it is your first day, and I hate to do this, but I have a doctor's appointment." I almost ask if everything is OK, but think better of it. "I hope I can trust you two here alone?" She stares at us in a way that makes me think it is less about her trusting us and more about her being able to see into our very souls and that she'd absolutely know if we stepped out of line.

"Yes, ma'am," I say, fighting an urge to curtsy.

Customers trickle in. Someone asks for enoki mushrooms, someone else wants a jar of Chanterelle's calming tea, and a couple in their late twenties order coffee and ginger snap biscuits and they make themselves comfortable at one of the far tables.

Then a tall man with a long brown beard walks in, and as soon as he does I feel the energy in the air change. He's almost twitchy, looking over his shoulder like someone might be following him, and when he approaches the counter, he won't make eye contact. As far as I know, Chanterelle doesn't sell anything exactly *illegal*. Hard to come by, strange, possibly icky, but all above board.

As far as I know.

"I heard I can get snake hearts here," he says, hands in his pockets, eyes darting around.

Ah. Chanterelle told us this might happen. I don't know why snake hearts are any stranger than chicken hearts or any other kind of animal heart that people can get, but apparently Chanterelle's is the only place for miles around where you can get them. She showed us them, pickled and in jars. It made my skin crawl.

"We sure do." I put on as much of a customer-service smile as I can muster. "How many would you like?"

The man looks up for the first time. "Are they still beating?"

My own heart picks up pace. *What?*

Amy pauses from making a pot of herbal tea and steps closer to me. "The snake hearts are in jars. So no."

I squeeze her hand behind the counter, glad she's here. She squeezes back three times: one long, two short.

The man sighs, clearly disappointed. "I guess that's better than nothing," he mutters. He scratches his head, doing some sort of calculation. "I'll take three."

"Wait one moment, please." Amy heads into the back store-room where Chanterelle keeps her more unusual ingredients.

"That will be ninety dollars," I say. Which seems both expensive and cheap for snake hearts.

The man fumbles with his wallet.

Then something catches my eye outside.

No, not something. Someone.

I recognize that shock of white blonde, almost silver hair.

It's her. The girl from the Revelry, the girl from the forest.

I'd started to think I'd dreamed her up, but there she is. Right outside Chanterelle's. She's real. I have to go see her.

"I'll be right back," I murmur to the man with the long beard as he frowns into his wallet, and I run outside, worried that I might miss the silver-haired girl. She's standing at the edge of the woods, like she's waiting for something.

I wonder if she's waiting for me.

"Hey!" I jog over to her. "What are you doing here?"

She smiles. "Bitsy! What a pleasant surprise. Wasn't expecting to see you here."

I ignore the pang that she wasn't here to see me. She eyes my apron that Chanterelle makes us wear. "And you work at Chanterelle's?" She begins to laugh. "What a marvellous coincidence. I used to work with Chanterelle."

I've never seen her at Chanterelle's. I'm here a lot with my grandma, so I'm surprised I haven't.

"Does she still stock the snake hearts?"

I nod. The girl shakes her head, still laughing to herself.

"Do you want to come in?"

The girl snaps her head up. "Oh, I wish I could. But I can't."

I wait for her to elaborate. She doesn't. Then her grin sharpens. "But you know what would be great? Could you pick me up a few things from the shop? Bring them to the woods..." Her voice trails off. "Where we met last time. If I'm not there, just leave them on the couch."

I nod, overeager like a Labrador. I don't want to let her down. I want to impress her.

She rattles off a few ingredients. Pink sea salt, dried seaweed and dried duck tongue.

"Duck tongue?" I make a face. "What for?"

But instead of explaining, the girl raises her chin and gestures over my shoulder. "Looks like someone is looking for you," she says in a sing-song.

I glance behind me. Amy is striding out of Chanterelle's, and she's scowling. When I turn back to the girl, she's still grinning. "See you in the woods."

Then she slips into the darkness of the trees.

A hand pulls at my arm. It's Amy. "Bitsy! What the hell?" Amy is breathing heavily. "I came out of the storeroom and you were just gone! And that guy, the weird one who asked for the snake hearts, he was acting super strange, and he took the hearts and left, and then that couple who asked for the cookies said he hadn't paid!" Her voice catches and I can tell she's about to cry. Oh shit. Reality comes crashing in. What was I thinking?

"I can't believe you just left like that!" She looks into the woods. "Who were you talking to?"

I don't know how to explain the silver-haired girl. How to explain that she was at the Revelry and she feels like my only link to what really happened that night.

I don't know if I want to share her.

"Sorry," I say. "I … thought I saw someone I knew. But it was just a friend of Chanterelle's." Not quite a lie.

"So you just ran out." Amy's mouth flattens into a thin line and I know she's pissed.

"I said I was sorry."

Amy holds her hands up. "You can apologize to Chanterelle for the missing ninety dollars. That isn't on me."

Chanterelle is furious.

"Let me get this straight," she says. "You left the shop unstaffed and someone left without paying for their items?"

"He said he'd paid," said Amy. "I didn't realize Bitsy had left the shop without making sure he'd paid."

I feel like we were carrying a couch and she's dropped her side, leaving me to lift it on my own. I hoped that maybe she'd take some of the blame.

And even though I know I should be a big girl and take responsibility – it is my fault, I know that – guilt brings out the worst in me. I don't usually do things that make me feel guilty.

"I didn't think that Amy would hand over ingredients to a customer without making sure he'd paid," I say. My finger begins to burn. I press my thumb to it. Why now? Maybe something in the shop irritated my skin.

Chanterelle sighs deeply and presses her fingers to the bridge of her nose. "Don't let anything like this happen again. I'm disappointed in you both. I'll be docking that ninety dollars from both your paychecks. Forty-five each."

Amy yelps. "But it was Bitsy's fault…"

Chanterelle looks at me sharply. "Bitsy, I'll leave it to you. Forty-five from you both or ninety from you?"

"Come on, Bits," says Amy quietly. I know she wants me to take all the blame, but it was on both of us. Maybe not exactly fifty-fifty, but I'm not going to be the only one who gets punished.

"Forty-five each seems fair," I say.

Amy sucks on her teeth so loud I flinch. Chanterelle raises a brow. "If you say so," she says. "I'll see you both next week. And I expect you to be on your best behaviour. If you disappoint me again, that's it, you're fired. No more chances."

We slink out of the shop.

In the car, Amy won't talk to me. She won't even look at me. She puts on her headphones and stares resolutely out of the window. It's only when I pull up in front of her apartment that she rips out her headphones in a savage motion and turns to glare at me.

"That was so screwed up of you."

"Why are you blaming me? You were the one who handed over the jar of hearts."

"Are you really not going to apologize?"

I don't say anything, because I'm scared if I do, I'll say something I'll regret. Something that will crack our friendship even further.

"Who even was that?" Amy goes on.

"You saw her, right?"

"What? Of course I did."

I hadn't realized how worried I was that I was imagining things until that very moment.

"She is real then," I muse.

"Bitsy! Stop changing the subject. Of course that person was real. Just like that forty-five dollars is real."

"This is bigger than that, Amy! She's from the Revelry! This is my first real clue into what happened that night."

"Oh, come on, Bitsy, let it go. It was a stupid party. I don't know why you are so obsessed with it!"

"Because weird things have been happening ever since then!"

"Like what?"

"Like … like my dress!"

Amy rolls her eyes. "You're being ridiculous. Ridiculous and selfish. You know I need that money from Chanterelle's to pay for make-up and costumes for Drama Club."

"Oh shit. I'm sorry," I say. And I mean it. It wasn't about the money for me. I wanted to share the blame. I didn't want to be the only one Chanterelle was disappointed in. Although it felt like she was almost more disappointed in me when I said that we were both at fault.

"I'll give you the forty-five dollars," I say.

"I don't need a handout," Amy snaps. "That was money I earned."

Amy and I don't talk about money very much. When we were younger, she used to come on vacations with me and my family. She stopped when she was old enough to realize that my parents were the ones paying for her to come.

"I'm sorry," I say. "I'm sorry for running out, and for saying we should split the difference. I just didn't want Chanterelle to put all the blame on me…"

"Even though it was your fault," says Amy flatly.

"I'm giving you the money! And I really am sorry."
I hold out my hand. "Forgive me?"

Amy sighs loudly. "Fine," she says. "I forgive you. But
don't pull that shit again, OK?"

"I won't," I say, still holding my hand out.

Amy squeezes my hand. "You know I hate fighting.
But, you were wrong here."

"Yes, yes, you can stop rubbing it in."

Later, when I'm in bed, and can't sleep, I text her.

Hey. Sorry again.

It's fine. Seriously.

**But you're right. I am obsessed with the Revelry. I can't
stop thinking about it.**

**Bitsy, let it go. Nothing happened. We danced. I think
there was a bonfire. What more is there to know?**

Of course! How could I have forgotten the bonfire?
Another memory slots into place. Huge flames, a crowd
all around us.

**You remember the bonfire! Do you remember what
happened to our togas?**

What?

I think our togas caught fire I type. And then, my
fingers move as fast as my thoughts. **I think someone
pushed us in the fire.**

Amy's response is immediate.

Bitsy, I love you, but you are being ridiculous. We would remember if we had been pushed into a fire. They probably stank from the bonfire smoke and were trashed from all the dancing. The material was cheap.

I start to type more, to tell her that I think she's wrong, that something happened, but she sends another message first.

Nothing bad happened at the Revelry. Now go to sleep.

And I want to push back. But I know how these things go. In Ember Grove, you don't question the strange. And if good luck comes your way, you grab it and are grateful. You definitely don't question where it came from. Apparently I'm supposed to do the same with bad luck. Because maybe Amy is right. And that is all this is. A bit of bad luck. I exhale and reply.

OK. I type. **Goodnight.**

It takes me a long time to fall asleep, and when I do, my dreams are full of fire.

Eleven

I go visit Grandma Shirley the next morning.

I'm unsettled from the fight with Amy, from seeing the silver-haired girl. But Grandma Shirley always grounds me.

"Hello, dear," she says as I come in. She's in her kitchen making a cup of tea, gazing out at the apple orchard through the window. "Do you want some tea?"

"I'm fine," I say. I nod out the window at the apple trees. "How are the apples?"

"Ah, gorgeous as ever. They do bring me so much joy. Did you know I loved apples even before we got into the business?"

"You might have mentioned it once or twice," I say and give her a kiss on the cheek. She smells, as always, of apples herself.

"But enough about apples for now," she says, turning to me with a twinkle in her eye. "I'm going to call in that favour."

"What favour?"

"You said you'd drive me anywhere I asked, remember?" She gives me a sly smile.

I start to laugh. "So, New York City?"

"Tempting. But not today. I was hoping to go get my hair done. Would you be a dear and drive me to my appointment?"

Even though my Saturday has now been commandeered by my grandma's hair appointment, I don't mind. "Of course."

We go to the only salon in town: Helen's Hair. Run by Ellen Helen and her two sisters. Ellen Helen has three daughters, and they all go to Ember High. One is in the year above me, and two are younger, so I don't know them super well. But I know *of* them, because everyone knows the Helen girls – and *everyone* knows about their hair.

They have the kind of hair that you see in shampoo commercials. Long and glossy, the kind of hair that you want to run your fingers through.

The kind of hair that the girl from the Revelry has, now that I think about it. I knew it looked vaguely familiar. The Helen girls don't have silver hair, they all have various shades of auburn, like Disney Princesses, but that shine is the same.

As we pull up in front of the salon, my grandma turns to me. "Ellen was at your dad's Revelry. Did you know that?"

This is a strange thing to say. I don't know why she said it like that. Not, *Ellen was in your dad's year at school.*

My grandma keeps talking as we get out of the car. "She'd been wildly in love with your dad's best friend. Oh, I can't remember his name now. He left Ember Grove, never came back. Teddy! That's it. Teddy Reed. Handsome boy, that Teddy. They broke up after their Revelry, I remember." She shakes her head a little. "Revelry always changes everything. You'll see, when you go next year."

"Grandma, I—" But right as I'm about to tell her that I did go to a Revelry, and I think everything has already started to change, someone blares their horn on the street next to us, drowning out my voice.

My grandma winces at the sound. "Good lord! What is wrong with some people?"

I know better now than to try to tell her again. I just shake my head along with her, watch the car drive off, then walk her into the salon. Inside, I take more notice of Ellen Helen than I ever have before. I remember the rumours that the Helen girls all have different dads. That Ellen Helen can't keep a husband. Watching her paint colour on someone's hair while telling a story, I wonder if it isn't that she can't keep a husband, but that she doesn't want to keep one.

Maybe her one true love was Teddy Reed, who never came back after the Revelry.

Revelry Revelry Revelry, it all comes back to the Revelry in Ember Grove.

My grandma won't be out of the salon for a few hours, but instead of driving home and coming back to pick her up, I decide to head to the Ember Grove Library. As I pass by the Founder's Fountain, I toss in a penny, then another.

When I'm out of pennies, I toss a nickel. Then a quarter. I even reach for a dollar, but I stop myself. Paper money would simply disintegrate. Silly to put it in. Silly to put any money in probably, but still. And I'm not the only one who feeds the Founder's Fountain.

Strangely, no matter how many pennies are tossed in there, you only ever see a few on the floor of the fountain. Which is weird, because I know I've tossed in hundreds over the years. I think kids, or maybe even adults, come at night and fish the pennies out. At least, I hope that is what happens. The library is quiet. More than quiet. Sounds in here are muffled, like the whole thing is wrapped in cotton wool, drinking up sound like a bandage soaking up blood.

Even though I couldn't find anything on the Revelry on the internet, maybe I'll be able to find something here.

I ask the stern librarian, who has been here my whole life, where I could find old newspaper clippings from the *Ember Grove Gazette*. She points me to a huge stack of old and yellowing newspapers at the back of the library and tells me to be careful not to damage any. I take a stack and carry them to a desk in the corner, and as I do, I pass a man scribbling away on his own pile of paper.

When I see who it is, I get a pang in my chest. James Sutcliffe. He's an author, world famous, but he can't remember his own name any more. He still writes his stories, and his wife sends them to his publisher, but he doesn't know who she is. Who *he* is. I watch him for a moment, and he seems completely lost in his own fictional world, in a strangely peaceful way.

But stranger things have happened in Ember Grove.

And that is what I'm looking for, I decide as I sit down at the desk, spreading some of the papers out in front of me.

I need proof of the strangeness, proof that it is linked to the Revelry.

Almost an hour has gone by and I haven't seen anything to do with the Revelry. But then a name pops out at me.

Florence Lonsdale.

The girl who never made it home from her Revelry.

It's her obituary, dated late summer, seven years ago. Her mom wrote it. I read it hungrily, feeling like a ghoul.

It doesn't mention the cause of death. It says she loved to sing and dance. It says she loved Ember Grove. And it says she wanted to open a dance studio here. And then, right at the bottom, it says, *"She spent her last night alive doing what she loved most: dancing the night away."*

It doesn't say at the Revelry. But I know that must be what it means. I hear Amy's weird sing-songy voice in my head. *"There was dancing. I remember dancing."*

I keep looking. More frantic now. I keep it up until it is time to meet Grandma Shirley, and then I drop her off at home and drive straight back to the library.

I read about more missing people, scan more obituaries, going back about 140 years. There are the expected deaths, old age and disease, that kind of thing, but so many of the articles are dated late summer. And I begin to notice that in those, the gap is always seven years. It reminds me of a rhyme we all used to sing when we were younger.

Seven trees for seven wishes
Seven hearts for seven kisses
Seven deaths for seven dreams
Seven stitches in seven seams
Try to jump from six to eight
Because seven is where you'll meet your fate

A chill runs up my spine. And the strangest thing about the obituaries every seven years is that the people are young. Teenagers. Seventeen or eighteen. Just graduated high school. One piece in particular catches my attention. A boy disappeared the summer my grandparents graduated high school. The summer of their Revelry.

I pause and count. Twenty-one names, twenty-one people who never came back from their Revelry. And the last one was Florence Lonsdale, seven years ago. And now, I can't help wondering – who's next?

Twelve

The Revelry is all I can think about.

No matter what I'm doing. At school, at the café, in the swimming pool. I'm on high alert all the time, trying to see if anything will jog my memory of what happened. To see if anyone else knows anything.

And then I start asking questions. Not about the Revelry itself, I know that won't work. I know my voice will stop, I'll start to cough or something. But I try to reach anyone who might have been at this year's Revelry.

I don't know everyone who would have been there, but I go through my yearbook to see if any names seem familiar. There is a girl in my grade, Laura, who has a brother who would have been there. I make a point to find her between classes, and to ask her how he is. We aren't really friends, so she gives me a weird look, but says he's fine. He's gone to university in another state. At swim, I casually ask if anyone has heard anything about the graduating class. Any drama. I hear stories about couples who broke up, people who went travelling, and who went to what university. If anyone who graduated last year has stuck around in Ember Grove, I can't find them. And I'm relieved that everything seems OK. That nobody was hurt, nobody went missing.

But why can't I remember? I still can't shake the feeling that something happened, and I have to figure out what it was.

I go over to Grandma Shirley's in the evenings after I've done my homework and watch her shows with her. And I try, again and again, to bring up the Revelry. When that doesn't work, I ask her about Grandpa Alfred.

Grandma Shirley loves talking about him. She shows me pictures of their wedding, of when they were young and would host parties in the orchard.

And that's when I see her.

When I see the silver-haired girl. Or someone who looks exactly like her. It must be her grandmother. What a strange coincidence.

I point at her and ask my grandma who she is, eager to know more, even if it is just a name, but my grandma's eyes go fuzzy, and she says she can't remember.

116

I go back to the woods one night. To find the living room. But I can't find it. And I can't find the silver-haired girl from the Revelry either. So the strange ingredients she requested from Chanterelle's stay under my bed, wrapped up in brown paper and tied with white string. And I feel a strange sense of loss, like I dreamed her up, and now I'll never see her again. I want answers to what happened at the Revelry, but it is more than that: I liked spending time with her.

I hope I'll see her again. But I don't know how. For all I know, she's already left Ember Grove. Maybe she's the one that's gone – and I'm the only one who remembers her…

At school, during lunch or between classes, I find myself floating on the edges. I've known everyone almost all my life, but I never clicked with anyone until Amy moved to Ember Grove.

But sometimes it feels like Amy clicks with everyone. She flits around, from Mark to Cecily to her Drama friends to the cheerleaders, laughing, knowing all the inside jokes and all the gossip and I want to ask her how she knows all this if I don't? There's an ease in how she carries herself around our friends that I know I'll never have.

And I guess the thing that matters is, Amy, the person who everyone wants to be close to, who everyone wants to be friends with, picked *me*. She wants to be friends with me. That has to mean something, right?

Right now she's sitting in the bed of Mark's black pick-up truck. The back is down and her legs dangle in the air as she tosses Skittles up for Mark to catch in his mouth like a trained seal. They're both laughing like it is the funniest thing that has ever happened, and I feel like I'm watching it a step removed, like there is a screen between me and them, like it's a film that I'm watching. There's a pep rally today, so Mark's in his basketball jersey, even though basketball season won't start up for a few months and Amy is wearing an old jean jacket and a leather mini-skirt, which shouldn't work so well but does. Like everything she wears. Even though they are *right* there, I can't get through.

But then Amy looks over at me, still laughing, and beckons me over, breaking that fourth wall that I put up, that I thought was so impenetrable.

"Bitsy," she cries out. "Come here!"

I obligingly walk over. "Bitsy," Amy says. "Mark says that the green Skittles are *apple* flavoured. They are clearly lime. What kind of messed-up taste buds does he have? I need you to back me up on this."

Mark is looking at Amy like she could say they were vomit-flavoured and he'd believe her, but then he laughs and shakes his head. "Nah," he says. "Definitely apple."

He grabs the pack out of her hands and tosses a green one at her. Amy catches the Skittle in question in her hand.

"You were supposed to catch it in your mouth," Mark says, doing just that to demonstrate.

"Your aim was off," says Amy, but she pops the Skittle in her mouth. "Lime! It's one hundred per cent lime!"

"It's apple."

"Here, find one for Bitsy. She can be the tie-breaker," says Amy.

I stand there, waiting for something to happen. Mark holds out the bag to me.

I don't even bother fishing around in the bag for a green Skittle. Instead I hold up the bag and scrutinize it. "Says here it's lime," I say dryly. I resist the urge to point out that they could have looked at the bag the whole time.

"Ah-*ha*!" Amy declares, jumping down and spinning around in a triumphant pirouette. "I knew it!"

"You would take Amy's side," says Mark.

"She always does," says Amy, blowing me a kiss.

And, for some reason, this grates. "Actually, the manufacturer of Skittles took your side."

Amy's face falls, just for a second, but then she recovers. "Oh, Bits," she says. "Always so logical."

"That's our Bitsy," says Mark.

Even though I'm still annoyed at them both, I find myself smiling. They've included me, and that's what I wanted, isn't it?

Steve ambles over. "What are you guys giggling about?" he says. I see Amy's eyes darting back and forth between me and Steve and I already know what she's thinking. I can see it projected out of her eyes like a video reel.

Double dates between the four of us: going to the diner on First Avenue and then to the drive-in, picnics in the glen, sunsets on Breaker's Hill. Never mind that practically nobody in our high school goes on actual dates, or that I'm not even vaguely interested in Steve – and he's definitely not interested in me. Amy thinks she can will this all to happen just by wishing hard enough. I know in her head, the only thing better than getting the boy she likes is setting up her best friend with said boy's best friend. It's thoughtful, in a way, but it also isn't. Because Amy's only thinking about what she wants, and not what I might want. Not at all.

Still. I offer the bag of Skittles to Steve. "Skittle?" He grins and pours the rest of the bag into his mouth, mashing them up in a multi-coloured rainbow in his mouth.

Mark laughs. "Bro!"

I manage a grin, pretending to be amused by the antics of a sixteen-year-old boy acting like he is six. The bell rings and Amy slides out of the truck and loops her arm through mine. "See you boys later," she calls out and pulls me through the parking lot.

"I saw how Steve was looking at you," she whispers in my ear, eyes bright with excitement.

I resist the urge to roll my eyes because I don't want to hurt her feelings.

"Liar," I say lightly. "You didn't see anything but Mark Lee's soulful dark eyes."

She laughs. "Shh! I don't want anyone to hear you." Then she sighs. "I swear it feels like there is … something between us. But maybe I'm imagining things."

"There is *definitely* chemistry between you two," I say.

We're outside my class, so I disentangle my arm from Amy's. "See you after school?" I say.

She shakes her head. "I've got auditions for *The Wizard of Oz*."

"Of course!" I exclaim. "Good luck – you'll be amazing."

That's one of her favourite musicals and she knows the songs by heart. She's made me watch it at least a dozen times during sleepovers. It is the perfect play for her to land the lead. "I know you'll nail 'Over the Rainbow'."

121

Amy smiles and rolls her eyes. "Bitsy, no offense, you always think my singing sounds great. You don't have a critical ear."

I lift a hand to my heart, mock-affronted. "Moi? I am an excellent judge of singing! Just you wait, I'll be sitting in one of those judging chairs."

Amy laughs and bumps her hip into mine. "To be fair, you have heard me sing more than anyone else on the planet. How many shows of mine have you been to?"

"I have literally lost count." And it's true. I've been going to Amy's shows ever since she was first cast as Annie when we were eleven. I go to opening night and closing, and I cheer the loudest.

"That's because you're the best," she says.

"I've got a big swim meet tomorrow, by the way," I say, hoping she'll take the hint and say she'll come. I know swimming isn't as exciting to watch as a play, but still. She doesn't come along often, but it's nice when she does.

"Well, good luck," she says. "Not that you need it." She pauses. "Do you want me to come watch?"

"That's OK," I say. Even though I *do* want her to be there. But I want her to come without me having to ask. "Watching swimming isn't like watching you perform."

"Well, just pretend I'm there in the crowd, cheering you on," she says, squeezing my arm. "I know you'll be the fastest one out there." I don't even think she knows my best time, but she has seen all the trophies my parents put on display in the front room. So she knows I'm fast, even if she doesn't know *how* fast.

"Thanks, Ames," I say. "Call me today, after your audition, and let me know how it goes."

But Amy doesn't call me that day after school. After dinner, I text her.

How did it go?

But no reply, even after she's seen the text. I hope that doesn't mean it didn't go well. Amy always replies to my texts. So I send a follow-up.

I'm sure you were AMAZING.

And then I send a bunch of dancing girl and heart and star emojis. By the time I've showered and got ready for bed, there is still no response. I don't want to pester her, so I just send one more.

See you tmrw morning?

That one finally gets a reply.

Of course! So sorry for radio silence – had a hectic afternoon, but GOOD! Tell you everything tmrw xoxoxoxo

I'm almost embarrassed at how relieved I feel that she's replied.

Thirteen

The next day, the clouds are low in the sky, and I feel like they are weighing down on the entire town. They are so full they look like they might burst. But Amy doesn't notice the weather. Amy is glowing when I pick her up.

"Bitsy, it was the best audition of my life. I've never sung like that before."

"I'm so proud of you!"

"Everyone else who was auditioning gave me a standing ovation," she says. "And then the rest of Drama Club insisted we go out after. I've never felt so confident about a performance. Like, I *nailed* it. I've *got* to be Dorothy."

I squirm in my seat, trying to squish the irrational jealousy rising up inside of me. That's why I didn't hear from Amy all afternoon. She was out with other friends.

I wait a beat to see if she'll apologize for ignoring me

all afternoon, but she's floating high in her successful audition bubble. And it stings. A lot.

That's why I say what I say next, because I want to puncture that bubble. Because it is a bubble I'm not in, and one that is carrying her up high, and away from me.

"But you aren't sure, right? Like, you won't know if you got the part until tomorrow?"

Amy shoots me a sharp look. "I mean, I won't know officially, but I'm feeling pretty good. Sometimes you just know, you know?"

I shrug, trying to remain calm even though my palms are starting to sweat on the steering wheel and I'm regretting what I've said. But it's like now that I've started I can't stop, like I've taken a step down a steep hill and there is no going back up – I can only barrel down, faster and faster, even though I know I'm going to lose my footing and end up in a heap at the bottom.

"I guess," I say. "I mean, at least with swimming we always know because it is pretty cut and dry: you either make the times you need to make, beat the other swimmers, or you don't. You always say how subjective acting is." And I feel mean, but also, I feel like it is true.

"Well, you'll just have to take my word for it when I say that my audition was great. Objectively so," Amy says. And then, "You wouldn't understand."

There is a rustling outside of our car, and without glancing out of the window, I know the trees will have leaned in as they like to do when Amy and I are fighting. As though they don't want to miss a single word.

I know I'm being bitchy and unsupportive and I hate myself for it, but it stings anyway. Maybe even more because I know it is my own fault. I wish I could rewind, drive in reverse and pull up in front of Amy's house again, and respond the right way when she tells me how well she did in her audition: cheer and demand that we go to the bakery for celebratory doughnuts.

I roll my shoulders back, trying to shake off this cloak of snarkiness that's descended on me. "Sorry. I don't know what I'm talking about when it comes to acting. It sounds like you killed your audition. I'm super proud of you. We should do something to celebrate after school today."

"No, you were right before," she says, sounding so glum that I know I succeeded in bursting her bubble, and now I regret it. "I bet I won't get Dorothy."

"No way. You definitely will," I say with as much conviction as I can, even though just thirty seconds ago I was doubting her claims that she had. It feels strange to be the one trying to lift her up – usually Amy is the positive one and I'm the voice of reason. But I want to cheer her up, especially because I'm the one who made her feel this way.

"Let's just wait to find out before we celebrate," she says.

"Good idea," I say. And then, trying to link us together, "And this way we can celebrate you getting the part and me hopefully getting my best time ever. Double celebration."

A pointed pause. "Yeah," she says. "If I make it. And if you win at your meet." The "if" makes me bristle, but I don't have a comeback because she's just doing what I did to her.

Amy and I barely speak all day. It's not that she ignores me exactly, but at lunch she's with Mark and Cecily, and I hover around the edges, laughing when I should, but not chiming in.

"Good luck this afternoon," Amy says with a smile when lunch is over. It's her real smile, so I know she means it. And I'm surprised by how relieved I am to see that smile. Even if things were a bit awkward in the car this morning, she still wants me to do well.

"I will do my best to swim fast and in a straight line," I say solemnly, and her grin widens.

"You'll be great," she says, squeezing my hand. "And then we'll go celebrate!" And the smile and her enthusiasm, and her belief in me, is how I know that everything between us is OK, that it's fine.

After school, on my way down to the pool, I pass the theatre where I know Amy is waiting to find out what part she got and I blow a kiss for good luck, even though I know she can't see it.

The school pool is at the back, behind the science labs. It's a huge outdoor pool with benches lined up on either side for people to watch from. Later this year, there will be college scouts on those benches, keeping an eye out for the best swimmers on the team. And I'm determined to be one of those. Scouts don't bother watching unless you are on varsity. On the top team. So today matters. A lot.

Once I've changed into my swimsuit and am waiting for my race, I'm hit by a wave of anxiety. I'm much more anxious than I thought I'd be. More anxious than I *should* be. I bounce back and forth on my bare feet, feeling the cold, wet concrete beneath my toes. My hair is pulled back and stuffed under a swim cap, and it feels tighter than it usually does. I pull my goggles down over my face, and wait for my race to be announced.

Part of me wishes I had taken Amy up on her offer to be here today, or maybe even asked my parents, but it isn't an official race. Just try-outs. Still, people have shown up to watch.

I feel strangely alone.

Then it's time.

I slice through the water, turning my head left then right, breathing in deeply when I'm above the water line. All I can see is the splash of the water in the lane next to me, the bobbing white buoys separating us, and the wall – the wall that means I've finished this lap – up ahead. I push harder. This meet is important. If I swim well enough, fast enough, I'll make varsity.

I'm dimly aware of people cheering, people lined up on the edge of the pool and in the stands, but only when I come up for air. When I'm in the water, it's a cacophony of legs and arms propelling forward, that low distorted thrum of solid bodies breaking through a liquid repeatedly, the sound seeming to come in slow motion by the time it hits my ears.

And then, just as I'm coming up to the wall to kick back, the water changes.

It doesn't feel like water any more. I'm swimming in mud. Thick, heavy mud that pushes me down. I start to panic and flail, invisible hands have grabbed my ankles, pulling me beneath the surface. My eyes are open behind my goggles and I can see the water is still clear, it still *looks* like normal water. But I can't go forward, I can't go upward – the thickness of the water is pushing me down, lower, lower, lower.

And suddenly I'm not in the pool any more but in the black water of Lake Lost.

My toga is pulling me down, and there is fire everywhere, and I'm going deeper and deeper, and my lungs start to burn, and I'm trying to kick up and out but the water is so heavy. And I can't let go of Amy. I won't let go of Amy. The water is pushing me down. I need to keep going … keep going…

Wait. Where's Amy? I'm alone. And the water is clear and bright, not dark like the lake water at night. I blink behind my goggles. I'm not in Lake Lost.

I'm in a pool. At the bottom. My feet scrape concrete. I take advantage of having something firm beneath my feet and kick off with as much power as I can, straining for the surface. It's a deep pool and the water still feels so heavy, but I'm pushing and pushing and…

I explode out of the water, gasping and thrashing. Everyone is staring at me like I've had some kind of fit. Maybe I have.

I don't bother swimming to the end of the lane. I pull

myself up on the side of the pool, my limbs trembling with the effort, like I've just swum harder than I ever have in my entire life.

Someone helps me out of the water – a girl in the year below me; I don't know her name – and it feels like a million eyes are on me.

What happened what happened what happened…?

It's like I can hear their thoughts. Or maybe it is just my own, getting louder and louder with each passing second.

What happened what happened what happened…?

Anna, one of the girls on my team, rushes over and hands me a towel. I wrap it around my shoulders like a cape, and then rip off my swim cap, letting my damp hair tumble around my shoulders.

Anna is staring at me, eyes wide. "Bits! Do you need to sit down? You're white as a ghost."

I let Anna guide me to a bench, ignoring the concerned looks and questions pelted my way. I tilt my head back and stare up at the milky white sky, so full of clouds it almost looks cloudless. It's strangely bright, for a day when you can't see the sun.

My finger burns. I look down. My ring scar looks like it did when my dress unravelled – red and raised and angry.

Fourteen

The incident is chalked up to a combination of fatigue and hunger.

I don't tell anyone of course. About what I saw when I sank to the bottom of the pool. What I remembered. But now that the memory is back, I can't forget it.

Though I still don't know what happened at the Revelry.

Our coach is bewildered. And I genuinely believe her when she says how sorry she is that this means I won't be able to swim varsity at the next race. When I know there will be scouts there. If I swim fast enough in my next few races, I might get back on varsity, but for these races, nobody will see me – nobody who matters, anyway.

It stings almost as much as my ring scar does.

I don't text Amy. I don't want to call her with bad news when she's riding high on the success of her audition.

At dinner, when my parents ask how the meet went, the spaghetti in my mouth feels like it is expanding and expanding and leaves no room for my tongue, no room for me to speak. I chug a glass of water, forcing it down.

"Fine," I manage, and nod.

They exchange a look. "Does that mean you're on varsity?"

I shrug and start to cough up the water I've just drunk too fast. "Lots of fast swimmers this year," I lie.

I know if I try to tell them what happened, they won't believe me, it won't make sense. The water changed? It pulled and pushed me down till I was at the bottom of the pool? They'll think I'm losing my mind.

The refrain of *what happened what happened what happened?* looping on repeat through my head changes slightly.

*What is happening **to me** what is happening **to me** what is happening **to me**?*

Because something is happening and I don't know what.

Later, when the house is dark and quiet, and I'm in my bed, I toss and turn. Toss and turn. Toss and turn. My mouth is dry, too dry. Like I've been breathing smoke.

133

I'm so thirsty. I go downstairs and drink a glass of water, and then another, but it doesn't help. All it does is give me a bellyful of water that sloshes loudly around as I toss and turn in bed.

I want to get out. I want to breathe in the night air. I want to see the stars. I want to remember that I'm alive.

I want to know what happened to me at the Revelry. And I'll do anything to find out.

I have to find that girl. *See you in the woods*, she said. Like an invite. Like a dare.

I'm not afraid of my woods.

The woods are wide and wild, but I know them. And I'll find her.

Because this time, the woods will listen to me.

I grab the paper-wrapped parcel from under my bed, pull on a sweatshirt and slip out of the back door. The clouds are covering the moon and it's so dark I have no shadow. But my feet carry me to the end of the orchard. Where the woods begin.

Last time we met in the woods it felt like a dream.

This time, maybe because it is more purposeful, everything is sharp edges and seen in stark relief. I feel like I'm watching myself in a film. Like I know what's going to happen even before it does.

The woods welcome me with a soft sigh. The branches caress my shoulders and the earth feels soft and springy beneath my feet. I hurry through the trees, careful to watch my step, following some sense I've never paid attention to before. I hope it is leading me the right way. Leading me to the living room. Leading me to *her*. I walk and walk and walk and there is no sign of the living room and no sign of the girl. No sign of anyone.

These are my woods. They won't play tricks on me like they might on some people. "Come on," I say, out loud. "I don't want to be out all night." The leaves above me rustle in the wind, letting through a shaft of pale moonlight. There, a narrow path I hadn't seen before. I put my hand on the nearest tree. "Thank you," I whisper.

The path eventually leads me to the living room. At first I think it's empty, but then I spot silvery blonde hair.

The girl from the Revelry is stretched out on the couch. Like she owns the place. Not just the couch but the whole forest.

I expect her eyes to be closed. I expect her to be sleeping because it is the middle of the night, but her eyes are open and she's staring right at me. Like she's been waiting for me.

"Well aren't you a brave one," she says. "Coming into the woods at night on your own."

"Do you … live here?" I say, glancing around the forest living room.

She laughs. "Not exactly. But I've been camping out here the past few nights."

"Don't you have parents?" I wince as soon as the words are out of my mouth. Maybe she *doesn't* have parents. After all, Amy doesn't. Not really.

She laughs again. "They know where I am. Don't worry about me. Sweet though. But that's you all over – sugar and spice and everything nice?"

I bristle. "I'm not a cookie."

"Well, Bitsy-not-a-cookie, what brings you to my neck of the woods?" She stretches out on the couch like a cat, clearly pleased with herself. Languid, like she has all the time in the world.

I hold out the parcel. "You asked me to bring you this, didn't you?"

She yawns and sits up, reaching for it. "Took you long enough."

"I couldn't find this place," I say as I step closer to hand her the parcel.

"Then you must not have wanted to find it."

I blink, and then realize she's right. Tonight I was desperate to find it, to find her. And then I did.

She unties the parcel. Opens the salt.

136

"What's your name?" I ask.

"What is this? Twenty questions?"

"I brought you what you asked for. You could at least tell me your name. It feels weird to be seeing someone for the third time and not know their name."

"Cute that you're counting how many times we've met," she says. Then she pours some of the pink salt directly into her mouth. I wrinkle my nose and she notices, pausing what she's doing to wink at me. "I've got a salt deficiency," she says by way of explanation. Then she starts to gnaw on the strips of seaweed. "And fair enough. I suppose you've earned the right to my name. My mother named me Summer … but I go by Skyler now."

"Skyler," I say the name tentatively, tasting it. It crackles on my tongue. It suits her more than Summer. I look up at the dark leaves overhead. "Sometimes I wish I had a different name. But everyone already knows me as Bitsy. And here in Ember Grove, that's all I'll ever be: Bitsy Clark."

"And why is that such a bad thing, Little Bits?"

She's looking at me like she actually cares, like she wants to know. And it feels good to be the focus of someone's attention. To have someone want to know me.

"Come, sit," she goes on, patting a spot on the couch next to her.

So I sit with her and I talk. First I tell her how I didn't swim well at the meet, and she nods sympathetically and listens and even sits up and pats my hand in a kind of soothing way. And then I keep talking. I tell her things I've never said out loud, that I didn't even realize I felt until I'd said them. I tell her about how, recently, it feels like Amy and I are starting to fray like a well-worn and well-loved blanket. I tell her about issues we've been having, the ones that I know are there but am not sure how to fix, because they're fickle, and move around like underwater currents, pushing us this way and that, and I don't know how to correct our course. How it feels like she would rather be with her Drama Club friends. How sometimes I wish I did Drama with her. How sometimes I'm jealous that people go watch the school plays but nobody wants to come to the swim meets. I've never said that to anyone. Not even to myself.

I tell her the thing that has been burrowing in my mind with sharp teeth and claws. About how good things are happening to Amy, and nothing good is happening to me. How it is starting to feel as though we're bound together in a way I don't like, and there is only so much luck between the two of us.

And Amy is getting it all.

The words spill out, like Skyler's broken-mirror eyes

have me in a trance. I shouldn't be surprised when she yawns and holds up her hand, wordlessly telling me to stop, but I am. I fall silent, and wait. I didn't know I needed to say all of this. I didn't even know I felt this way until I said it.

She shakes her head a little, like she's clearing it out. Clearing me out. "Well," she says on an exhale. "That's quite a lot."

"Sorry," I say, suddenly embarrassed and leaning back against the prickly couch. I close my eyes so I don't have to see her expression. "I don't know why I went on and on like that."

"No, don't worry about it," she says, and her voice is so warm I open my eyes again. She's smiling at me in a way she hasn't before, like we're friends. I feel like I've earned that smile, and it feels good. "You clearly had a lot to get off your chest. And I get it. I really do. Friendships are tricky. But I'll be honest, Bitsy, it doesn't sound like Amy is as good a friend to you as you are to her. It sounds like she takes you for granted."

It's like I've been waiting for someone to say those exact words, because hearing them opens a box in my brain with that very thought locked inside and now it's jumping around and shouting and *yes yes yes I am a better friend*. Things aren't always equal between me and Amy.

She *does* take me for granted.

Skyler is right.

"But that's OK," Skyler goes on, unaware of how my brain is spilling out all these thoughts I've never let myself think before. "High school doesn't last for ever. And in the meantime, you don't have to be joined at the hip with your little bestie. You can have other friends, you know."

The *you know* lingers in the air. Like an invitation.

I feel like I've been chosen. Like I'm special. This strange, striking, mysterious girl wants *me* to be her friend. She wants to take me under her wing.

Not Amy. Even though Amy has purple hair and can get on a stage and sing in front of hundreds of people and can make anyone laugh.

Skyler wants to be friends with *me*.

Fifteeen

I end up staying out with Skyler until sunrise. We talk and talk and she tells me about bands I've never heard of, and gossip about the town that I didn't know, and the secrets of the woods. She tells me to watch my step after a thunderstorm when the ground is wet and springy, because the skeletons stir. How anything whispered in the woods is remembered for ever, so never say a secret when the trees might be listening. It reminds me of when I was little, before Amy, when I would roam the woods alone. When I felt like the trees themselves were my friends. It feels like coming home.

"How do you know all of this?" I'm a little breathless with awe at it all. With her.

"A friend told me," she says with that sly smile. "And now I'm telling you."

When I stumble out of the woods and into my orchard, the sun is cresting across the horizon, lighting the world up. I'm exhausted but exhilarated. When I was in the woods with Skyler, I felt like I could stay up all night, like I didn't need sleep, like I'd never need it, but now I feel like I could sleep for one hundred years. I collapse into bed, humming a song that Skyler had been humming as we walked through the woods, the tree branches tangling in the moonlight above us.

The tune is strangely familiar…

And then, right before sleep pulls me under, I remember.

Amy was humming it.

It is the song from the Revelry.

I sleep until noon. A deep sleep. If I dream, I don't remember and when I wake up, my skin feels tight. Like it's stretching to contain this new person I am becoming.

My parents have let me sleep in because it is Saturday and I don't have a swim meet. A rare thing. I almost never sleep this late.

I roll over in bed and grab my phone and frown. I have *seventeen* messages from Amy. I look at them, blinking and twinkling on my phone, and think of what Skyler said. That Amy isn't being a good friend to me.

I think about how I didn't even want to tell her about what happened to me at my swim meet.

And, for a moment – and I hate myself for it – I hope that she hasn't got the part. That she'll need me to comfort her. That we can rage against the unfairness of everything together. We'll be on the same side, our fates linked but in the same way, our happiness and luck shared.

But then I open the messages.

OMG! OMG! OMG! BITSY!

GUESS WHAT?!?!?

OMG I GOT IT! DOROTHY! I'M THE LEAD!

AHHHHH!!

THOSE RUBY RED SLIPPERS ARE MIIIINE!

I'm going to be a STAR, baby!

More of the same. Then:

Bitsy? Helloooo where are you?

And finally:

Cecily wants to celebrate. (So sweet, right?) She's got family stuff today so tomorrow afternoon?

I swallow my disappointment at her good news and the annoyance that Cecily is out-friending me. I don't want to feel like this, but I can't help but be glad Amy told me over text and not in person, so I don't have to have the right face.

OH MY GOD I KNEW YOU WOULD!!

I reply.

SO PROUD OF YOU!

And both of these things are true. I did know, in my heart, that she would. And I am proud of her.

But I can't shake the feeling that I lost my place on varsity because she got the part. It slithers in under my skin like a slippery eel that I can't catch, thick and fat and slick with sharp teeth.

Maybe maybe maybe, it hisses.

Maybe there really is only so much luck to go around.

Or *maybe maybe maybe*.

Maybe it is more than that.

I look at the scar on my finger. The one that matches Amy's. Red and raised and ugly. And I have a feeling that the scar on her finger is smooth. Instead of tying us together, our luck feels like it's pushing us apart. Like when something good happens for Amy, it's bad for me.

But no, that is ridiculous. It's just a silly scar on my finger.

From a night I can't remember.

I swallow again and push down the eel beneath my skin, rubbing the scar with my thumb.

Amy deserves this, I tell myself. The eel inside of me shakes its head. *She does,* I tell it sternly.

I text again, saying just that.

And of course I want to come celebrate with her, but I'm irrationally hurt that Cecily is the one organizing it. Shouldn't I be the one doing that? Did she tell Cecily before me?

But then I check the time stamps. Three hours from when she first texted to when she said Cecily wanted to celebrate. That makes sense. And Cecily loves any excuse for a celebration.

But still it stings.

I realize I should call. This is a big deal for Amy. It deserves more than a text full of emojis and exclamation marks. And, she might think that I'm the one being a bad friend for taking so long to reply.

But … it all feels too much.

A lump rises in my throat and this isn't at all how I want to be responding. I want to be happy for Amy. But for some reason I can't be. This isn't like me. I'm always the one who is there to cheer her on. Maybe that is why this is hitting so hard. I need her to be there for me too. But I need to pull myself together. Be the friend I want to be. The one Amy expects me to be. So I take a deep breath, and call.

145

She answers almost immediately. "Why, hello!"

"Congratulations! You star!"

"Thanks, Bits. I'm so happy." But she sounds a little distant. And slightly annoyed. I know it is because I took so long to respond to her, but she can't expect me to be on call twenty-four hours a day. And it isn't like I was even the first person she told. She obviously told her friends from Drama first.

I have my own life too, I think. And strangely, I hear Skyler respond, telling me that of course I have my own life. I'm more than Amy's personal cheerleader.

"So what's the celebration plan for tomorrow?" My voice is bright but brittle, like tin-foil. I hope she can't tell that I'm on the verge of tears.

"This might sound weird, but hear me out. I was thinking we would actually go to Chanterelle's."

"Chanterelle's as in where we work?"

"I've reserved the Willow table."

She's already reserved a place?

"And it is kind of ideal because you are working tomorrow afternoon, remember?"

Oh. I'd forgotten.

"We can't do, like, breakfast somewhere instead?" I say.

"Cecily has plans in the morning."

Since when do we prioritize Cecily's schedule over mine? I don't say it, but it is like Amy heard me because she barrels on, voice defensive. "And since she was the one who suggested we all go out to celebrate..."

The dig is light but sharp. Like a thorn pricking your skin enough to sting but not draw blood. Cecily responded quickly. Cecily responded better. Cecily suggested celebrating while I hadn't responded at all.

Amy is telling me what I don't want to hear: Cecily is being the kind of friend she needs right now. And I'm not.

I roll my eyes, glad that Amy can't see me.

"Totally makes sense," I say in my tin-foil-bright voice.

"And if we go to Chanterelle's, you can still come." Amy wants a big celebration. And I know she thinks she's being thoughtful finding a way to include me.

"Makes sense," I say. Then because I can't help myself, "But we should do something else too, you know, just the two of us, when I'm not working. This is a big deal for you!"

Amy does this little huff laugh. "I was worried you didn't get it, like, what a big deal it is. Because, you know, you kind of ghosted me all day."

Again I'm glad she can't see my face. I ghosted *her*? She's the one who didn't respond to me after her audition.

Typical Amy, to make everything about her. And having a life apart from her doesn't make me a bad friend.

For a brief moment, I want to tell her about where I've been. I want to tell her about Skyler. About how she's telling me the secrets of the woods.

But I don't want to share. So instead I lie.

"I think I'm coming down with something. I went to bed early last night and didn't wake up until, like, just now."

I don't mention my swim meet. It's a silent test. I wait to see if she notices. If she asks. If she remembers the things that matter to me. But she doesn't.

"Hopefully you'll feel better tomorrow," she says.

Of course she believes my lie, because why wouldn't she? Bitsy Clark doesn't lie, doesn't stay out all night, doesn't have her own secrets to tell.

Even the night we went to the Revelry, the Revelry that changed everything, was Amy's doing. I wouldn't have gone on my own – and that's the Bitsy Amy thinks she knows.

But things have changed.

Sixteen

It's strange to be working when my friends are at the café.

The other person working with me this afternoon is Tony, who has worked here as Chanterelle's assistant for as long as I can remember. He's currently watering the plant wall. I scurry over to him.

"Tony," I say. "Do you mind keeping an eye on things for a minute? I'm going to go say hi to some friends."

He lifts a heavy eyebrow. "The friends who are sitting at the Willow table?"

"It's Amy," I say quickly. "She talked to Chanterelle and reserved it. Don't worry. And I'm just going to go take their order and say hi."

"Be quick," he says.

I beam at him and then hurry to the Willow table, pushing back the long branches to let myself in.

It is like going into a tiny wonderland. The table perches on the edge of a small pond beside the willow, which Chanterelle must have built the whole café around. The table itself is tiny and delicate. There is clearly only room for four around it. And Amy, Cecily, Tanya and Danielle are already sitting. I hover, not sure if I should grab another chair or what. Especially since, technically, I'm working.

Amy is bright-eyed and rosy-cheeked with excitement. "Bitsy! Here, squeeze in," she says, scooting over so she's half on her chair and half on Cecily's.

"Let me get the order first," I say. "I am working."

"I was just about to say, it is hard to toast Amy without any cups!" says Cecily.

"Yeah, I know. That's why I said I should get the order," I tell her, reminding myself that this is what Amy wanted for her celebration. She's what is important.

Rose and lavender teas all round, rose and lavender cookies too. I try to catch Amy's eye, because we always laugh at the customers who go all floral at the café, but she's already turned back to Cecily, and is telling her about the set design for the show.

So I walk away, out of the Willow, to go place the order. I can hear Amy and the other girls laughing, and even though I know they aren't laughing at me, the sound grates on my ears.

When I get back, balancing five hot teas and a tray-ful of cookies, they are still talking about the show. "Celebration cookies!" I interrupt with forced cheer. I place everything on the table and sit down, or more like perch, in the tiny space Amy's made for me.

"Careful, Big Bits," says Cecily. "Watch out for those branches." I force a laugh, even though I hate the nickname.

"Anyway, as I was saying," Cecily goes on, "Amy, I'm so proud of you. You're so talented. Seriously. We've got to get you discovered somehow. Like big-time discovered. Like bigger than Ember Grove High musicals. You should be on Broadway."

I'm surprised when Amy doesn't bat away the praise. "You know, I've been thinking maybe I should start shar-ing more of my singing online."

This is the first I've heard of that plan.

"Genius," says Cecily. "I can help. You know I've got a huge following." She holds out her hand to show her long nails painted pastel blue. "Guess how many people watched me do my nails last night?"

I'm trying to tune out Cecily as I take the first sip of my own tea when something skitters down my spine.

I whip my head around so fast I get a crick in my neck. "What the...?" I mutter, trying to see what it was.

"Bitsy, everything OK?" Amy says staring at me, not with concern, but more with embarrassment. Like I've embarrassed her with my behaviour. I feel the eel inside me start to slither around, mouth open, teeth sharp.

"Yeah, everything is fine," I say, turning back around. I force a smile. "All good."

Then a spider falls from my hair into my cup.

And another one. And another. And then it is an avalanche of spiders, falling from my hair all over the table. They're black and the size of dimes and there are so many of them, crawling out of my hair.

Cecily screams and leaps away from the table.

"Oh my God!" Tanya gets up so fast her chair topples over into the water beneath the willow tree.

And the spiders keep falling.

I'm so stunned I can't move. It's like I'm in a nightmare. The spiders keep coming, like they've nested in my hair and are now hatching. I can feel them crawling down my face, down my neck, but I'm frozen with horror.

Amy is smacking spiders off me as fast as she can and then I finally begin to move, shaking my hair out, jumping up and down, not caring how I look, just wanting to get the spiders *off*. Cecily and Tanya are still screaming and Danielle has disappeared.

Another one drops down into my field of vision and a Revelry memory overtakes me.

After the horn sounds, the girl with the silver hair disappears. And it is just me and Amy standing in the dark, dark woods. Me and Amy, staring at each other. Me wanting to go. Her wanting to stay. Our braided rings connecting us. And then we walked back towards the lake – because I wouldn't leave her, she knew it, I knew it – and I walked through a spiderweb. The gossamer strands clung to my face and my hair and two spiders crawled down my arm.

Go go go, the woods were telling me. My woods. But we didn't listen.

The willow branches sweep open like a curtain. Chanterelle is standing there with a face like thunder.

"What is going on?" she demands. Behind her shoulder I see other customers standing, trying to see what is happening at our table.

"She's infested!" Cecily shouts, pointing at me. She knocks off a glass and it shatters on the floor. "She's got spiders living in her hair!"

"I do not!" I say, eyes burning with unshed tears. "They must have been in the tree! They fell on me!"

"Silence!" says Chanterelle. "All of you!" She's so imposing that even Cecily shuts up.

I'm still trembling. Spiders are still crawling all over the table. Maybe even still crawling all over me.

Tony bustles in with a cleaning brush and bucket and calmly sweeps the spiders into it.

"Bitsy, go out with Tony," says Chanterelle in a voice that has no room for argument. "And honestly, ladies, all this screaming over a few little spiders. I'm especially surprised by you two," she says to me and Amy. "A spider or two shouldn't bother you. Goodness knows what you would do if you had to deal with the snakes."

Cecily blanches.

"Come on, Bitsy," says Tony gently. Back behind Chanterelle's, on the edge of the forest, Tony empties out the bucket of spiders at the base of a tree, and they scuttle off. Then he turns to me. "I should probably spray you with the hose, just to make sure there aren't any hiding on you."

I'm still so shell-shocked that I nod and don't move when he hoses me down like I'm an animal, blasting spiders out of my hair and off my skin, till I'm soaked. "Sorry, Bitsy," he says, not making eye contact with me.

"It's fine," I mumble, my teeth chattering. I look back at the café, waiting for Amy to come out, waiting for her to make sure I'm OK.

But she doesn't. She stays inside.

"You can go home," Tony says. "I'll finish the rest of your shift. You should shower. Get some rest." He pauses. "Maybe check your scalp. For bites and whatnot."

I start to shudder and can't stop.

"Hey, hey," he says soothingly. "You'll be OK. Weird things happen around here. Hell, that isn't even in the top ten weirdest things I've seen in Chanterelle's café. You're an Ember Grove girl, don't let this shake you."

I scrunch my eyes tight and nod. He's right; he's right. I need to brush it off. But I can't stop trembling.

When I get home, I'm still shaking as I peel off my wet clothes, searching for spiders, but only one dead one falls out of my sleeve. Then I get in the shower and turn the water up as hot as I can stand it and wash my hair again and again and again.

It's only when I'm drying myself off that I notice it.

My ring scar is burning again.

I wonder when it started.

I don't know what I was expecting from Amy, but it wasn't for her to show up unannounced. No texts, no calls.

But when the doorbell rings and immediately the door creaks open, I know it's her. She's had a key to our house for years, just like I have one to her apartment. I hear her saying hi to my mom, and my mom saying something back.

A few moments later, she bursts into my room and flops down next to me on my bed.

"I'm guessing you didn't tell your parents what happened," she says. "Otherwise your mom would have mentioned it."

I shake my head. How do I explain the unexplainable? That hundreds of spiders crawled out of my hair. That the school pool tried to drown me. That my dress tried to suffocate me.

"They don't know … anything." I say.

"Are you OK?"

I snort. "OK? No. Not really. And it isn't just this. The spiders. Weird things have been happening since …" I lower my voice, "… the Revelry." Even saying the word is hard. It burns coming out.

Amy glances down at her scar, almost as a reflex, but her ring scar is smooth. Not like mine. "Oh, Bitsy, you can't still be talking about that," she says. "Be rational. Everything has an explanation."

"Easy for you to say. Everything is fine for you." I can't keep the bitterness out of my voice.

Because it's true.

"Way to not be happy for me," Amy says, sitting up and away from me. "I came over here to check on you. I didn't have to, you know."

"Oh wow, I'm so lucky you care enough about me to make sure I'm OK after a truly traumatic and embarrassing incident," I snap back. But then I wilt. "It would be nice to feel like you were on my side." She hadn't even followed me outside. She'd just let me slink off on my own, like I had something to be ashamed of.

"Everyone knows I'm on your side! We're Bitsy and Amy. But that doesn't mean we need to wear matching friendship bracelets."

I don't want us to fight. I want us to go back to how we were over the summer, how we've been for years. I want us to be Bitsy and Amy, like she said. So I'm careful to lighten my tone. "*You* were the one who made us wear those in seventh grade, if I recall correctly."

"Those were custom-made," says Amy, mouth twitching like she might start laughing. "And very fashionable for seventh grade."

"I still have mine."

"You'd better!" She grins and, despite everything, I

grin back. But then her face grows serious. "Bitsy, that was terrifying."

"How do you think it was for me?"

"Do … do you know where they came from?" She leans closer and rubs my arm, almost like she's checking that they aren't there any more. Or maybe she's just trying to comfort me.

The couch in the woods flashes through my mind again. It must have been that. Right?

"I've been walking through the woods," I say. Not a lie. Just not the full truth. "Maybe a spider fell in my hair and laid her eggs."

Now Amy shudders. "Don't go in the woods on your own. You're the one who taught me that."

"I'm fine," I say, with a calm I don't feel. "Anyway, how was the rest of your afternoon?"

"Chanterelle was surprisingly relaxed after everything was cleaned up. And I heard her asking Tony if you were OK."

"Do Cecily and the girls think I'm some sort of filthy spider-wearing wretch?"

"I like how you say 'spider-wearing' like it was a fashion choice."

"You didn't answer my question," I say. "About what they think of me."

"I don't know why you care."

"Because they are meant to be our friends. My friends."

"They *are* your friends. Yeah, Cecily was being … well, she was being Cecily, but I could tell she was worried. And after you left she even asked when your next swim meet is."

Swim. I realize I haven't told Amy about what happened during the try-outs.

"What is it?" says Amy, poking me in the side. "What's wrong?"

"Something else weird happened," I say. And I tell her. About the water growing heavy all around me. How I lost my spot on varsity. "Like I told you, weird things keep happening to me."

"That *is* weird," says Amy. "But there has to be an explanation. Just like there's been an explanation for everything. You had an allergic reaction to the dress, you just said yourself that you think the spiders came from the woods, and the water…" Her voice trails off. "That sounds like anxiety, Bits."

"You don't understand! I couldn't swim!"

"I believe you," she says. "I just think … it isn't caused by some mysterious thing."

"That's because you aren't from here," I say, the words coming out sharper than I mean.

159

"Oh not this again," she says, rolling her eyes. "I *know* I'm not really from here. God knows you remind me enough. I moved here when I was eight, but it will never be enough to make me a *real* Ember Grove girl." Her tone is salty and sarcastic, but I can tell she's hurt. And I feel bad.

"Amy, I didn't mean that," I say. "I just mean, I don't think you take things seriously sometimes. Like everything that is happening to me. It's … weird."

"Weird is normal for this town, remember? You are the one who has always told me that. I work in a café that sells snake hearts, I believe stories about a porch full of snowy owls, and went to a party everyone goes to and no one talks about. But now you want an explanation? That isn't how things work in Ember Grove, and you know it." She exhales. "Let's try to get back to normal, OK? You and me, and … everything else." Amy stands and stretches. "On that note, your mom says I should stay for dinner. Your dad is making homemade gnocchi."

"So you're obviously staying," I say. Gnocchi has been her favourite since the first time she had it at my house.

"Of course," she says, with a wide grin. A grin that says, *"Hey, let's think about gnocchi and* The Wizard of Oz *and not any of the unpleasant things that keep happening to you."*

I can tell she wants to push everything, all the weirdness that has been happening to me, the weirdness between us, under the rug. No, not just under the rug. She wants to push it out of the window and hope that it blows far, far away.

And I play along, because what else am I going to do? I nod with excitement as she tells me about her upcoming rehearsal schedule, and how she's nervous about seeing Mark tomorrow because things feel different between them, but a good different, and how she hopes he likes her as much as she likes him, and also what song do I think she should do for her college audition piece?

She doesn't ask me anything about me. It is Amy, Amy, Amy. And I don't even want to talk about myself right now. I want to talk about the Revelry.

I feel like she's abandoned me, in a weird way. Like she led me to the Revelry, and left me there. I know she didn't *actually* leave me there, but in a way, she has. It makes me want to unravel the Revelry even more.

I know *something* is happening; I just don't know what it is. And I don't want to push it away; I want to figure it out.

I *need* to figure it out. Before anything else happens to me.

Seventeen

If Amy won't help me, I'll have to do it alone.

But when I go back to the library the next afternoon to see if I can find any more clues, the old archives I was looking through are gone. I ask the librarian what happened, and she says they've been sent out to be digitized and it will take weeks, maybe months.

I return home feeling discouraged, and I'm half-heartedly doing homework in my room, and helping Amy figure out what to wear via text, when something thuds against my window. I jump.

It's an apple.

What the hell?

Then another thump.

I open my window. Skyler is sitting in the top branches of the nearest apple tree, grinning at me, an apple in her hand.

"Did you just throw an apple at my window?"

"No, a little bird did." Skyler laughs, and the sound is warmer than usual. "Of course it was me."

"Why didn't you ring the doorbell like a normal person?" I say, but I'm grinning back. Skyler is showing me a whole side of Ember Grove I didn't even know existed. A whole side of myself I didn't know existed. It makes me feel like I'm one of those Russian nesting dolls, and I like it.

"Whatever gave you the impression I'm a normal person?" she says dryly. "Where've you been? You haven't come to the woods in a while."

"All of three days," I tease. "Did you miss me?"

"I wouldn't go that far. Has high-school life ensnared you again?"

I think of the spiders. I think of the fight with Amy. "Something like that."

"Want to talk about it?"

"How come you're so nice to me? Why do you even care?"

She shrugs. "I guess I see a little bit of myself in you. Now, are you coming down or not?"

A fuzzy, warm feeling runs through me. "Just give me a second." My parents are leaving when I get downstairs. They are going to dinner at a friend's. And then, just as they're walking out, my mom asks me where Amy is. I can tell she's wondering why Amy isn't where she usually is: with me.

"She's got plans." I don't know why, but I don't want my mom to know that she has a date with Mark. It isn't that I'm jealous, but I know it will make my mom wonder why I'm also not out on a date. When she was my age she had dates all the time.

"Oh, I thought she might be at rehearsal. So wonderful that she was cast as Dorothy. She's so talented. I can't wait to see the show."

"I hope you've told her how proud we are of her," adds my dad.

"I already did," I say. I think about how my mom only came to two of my swim meets last year. Out of eighteen. But she's seen all of Amy's shows. "Have a good night."

I find Skyler sitting in one of the trees. I expect her to come down, but instead she grins down at me. She looks as comfortable lounging in the apple tree as she does on the couch in the woods.

I want that – to look comfortable wherever I am. I want it to seem like the world stops for me.

Skyler carries herself like if she decreed it, the trees would halt their growing, the birds would quiet their song. She carries herself like a queen, and yet like someone without a care in the world, and, oh, I want to be like that.

"Tell me, Itsy Bitsy, what silly high-school problems plague you?"

"You'll laugh."

And she does, before I even say anything. "Of course I will. But I'll listen too."

So I tell her how I'm worried nobody will invite me to the homecoming dance and even though I don't want to care, I do. It shouldn't matter but it does. I want to have that experience, I want to go to the dance. I don't want to be left out.

And I tell her about how things are still strained between me and Amy. But that Amy doesn't even seem to notice, as long as I'm there being Supportive Friend Bitsy.

And I tell her about the spiders.

At this, she raises her eyebrows. "I wouldn't expect a spider or two to bother you."

"It wasn't just the one spider," I say. "There were … hundreds."

"You should have thrown back your head and laughed and called them your loyal subjects. These very woods could do your bidding, if you wanted."

I laugh now. "That wouldn't have gone down especially well. Maybe next time. Although I really hope that never happens to me ever again."

"And your friend, the amateur actress," and it is mean, but I smile at the way that Skyler says *amateur*, "she sounds positively clichéd. All obsessed with a boy who will mean nothing to her in a few years."

"For somebody who has only just graduated high school, you sound pretty dismissive of it."

"Home-schooled, remember? And I'm wise beyond my years. Trust me."

"I guess … it does all seem a little silly," I admit.

Skyler's eyes light up. "I have an idea. Now, I'm sure you'll end up going to your little dance – and you should. Go, be merry, but then," her smile spreads. "Come meet me in the woods! We'll have a party of our own. It will be far better than a sweaty gym filled with high-schoolers."

"Really?"

"I promise. You can regale me with tales of how awful the dance was and we can laugh at everyone and feel certain of our superiority."

"OK then," I say, excitement fizzing through me. It reminds me of how I felt the night that Amy and I snuck into the Revelry – the before, when it was all giddy anticipation.

"And you'll know where to find me."

"Up a tree?"

She gives me a look. "In our charming living room. You'll find it if you try hard enough. But remember —" her eyes grow stormy — "bring only yourself. I have zero interest in entertaining any other teenagers. You delight and amuse me. Others would not."

I mock-curtsy. "I aim to please."

"That's what I like to hear." Skyler pulls one of the apples loose, and takes a big bite. It crunches loudly and flecks fly out of her mouth. "These are good," she says, sounding almost surprised.

"Of course they are," I say, feeling oddly defensive of the apples. "They come from Clark Orchards."

She shrugs and takes another bite. "They'd better be good," she says. "Considering what they cost."

I frown. "What are you talking about? My grandpa bought this land cheap. Nobody thought anything could grow on it."

Skyler begins to hum that song again, the one from the Revelry. Did someone sing it? Was there a band? I know there was music — I remember the music, a bit — but the song feels different.

"Bitsy, who are you talking to?" It's Grandma Shirley, standing at her back door, looking out into the orchard and frowning. It is almost like Skyler has summoned her with the song. "I looked out of my window and I saw you talking to someone up in one of the trees!" She hobbles over, slowly and hunched over. She looks so small amongst the apple trees.

Then she catches sight of Skyler. She stops short and puts her hand on her chest. "Oh." The word falls from her mouth like a stone from a cherry. "*Oh.*"

Skyler swings down and lands softly on her feet. "You must be Grandma Shirley," she says. "Nice to meet you."

"What are you doing here?" says Grandma Shirley, suddenly fierce. "Why are you talking to my Bitsy?"

"I think you have me confused with someone else," Skyler says. She looks over at me with a sympathetic smile. "I know sometimes this happens: they get confused."

"I'm not confused! And I can hear you! I know who you are, but I don't know what you are doing in my orchard!" It takes me a moment, but then I realize Grandma Shirley is frightened. Skyler is right: she is confused. I take her arm.

"This is just a friend of mine," I say gently.

Skyler begins to hum the Revelry song.

Grandma Shirley's eyes begin to dart around. "Where's Alfred?" she says, sounding panicked.

"Grandpa isn't here, Grandma."

This has never happened before. Not in the four years since it happened has she forgotten that Grandpa has passed away.

Grandma stares at me, eyes wild. "The apples came after the Revelry. I didn't know. I didn't know what he'd said. What he'd promised. I just knew the apples started growing." My grandma begins to weep. "I didn't know what it cost."

I rub my grandma's back, trying to stay calm. "Grandma, you're OK. Come on, let's go inside. I'll make you a cup of tea." I've always wanted her to tell me about her Revelry, but not like this. Not if it makes her so scared and anxious.

"I would have said no! But I didn't know!"

I look at Skyler. "I don't know what she's talking about," I say, trying to keep my rising anxiety out of my voice. I'm starting to feel really worried about her. "I should get her inside."

But my grandma is pushing me off of her and pulling apples down from the low-hanging branches. The apples thud to the ground.

"Grandma!"

"I'd forgotten! I'd forgotten what happened. But now…" She turns and points at Skyler. "You were there! You knew!"

I expect Skyler to laugh or look away or look awkward. But instead she whistles a short, sharp whistle that makes my ears ring. I wince.

And my grandma stops moving completely. Her eyes glaze over and her jaw goes slack. An apple still in her hand rolls to the ground.

"What … what did you just do?" I stare at Skyler.

"Sometimes a high-pitched noise can shock someone out of a panic attack," she says calmly. Like my grandma isn't swaying on her feet next to us. It makes me feel like I'm seeing a brand-new side of my new friend, one that I don't think I like very much. "That or slapping them across the face. And I didn't think that was especially acceptable." Then she sighs. "It all makes sense now though. Apparently I'm a carbon copy of my own grandmother. And of course she was probably at the same Revelry as your grandma. I must have triggered some sort of memory in her."

"But why is she so upset?" I move closer to my grandma so she can lean on me.

"Hasn't she ever told you what happened at that Revelry?"

"Nobody ever talks about their Revelry – you of all people should know that." I'm surprised that the word is even coming to my mouth so easily.

"Oh, but this is something even a Revelry can't hide." Her teeth flash in a feral grin. "Somebody died that year."

I shake my head. "No, he disappeared."

Skyler purses her lips and *tsks* at me. "Or did somebody bury the truth?"

My grandma lets out a low moan, and then seems to snap out of her trance. "I didn't know!" she says, grabbing me roughly by the shirt. "I didn't know what he'd done until it was too late."

"Grandma! It is OK. It was a long time ago."

Grandma Shirley looks back at Skyler. "And she was there. And she knew exactly what was happening."

Skyler leaves after that. Disappears back into the woods, glancing apologetically at me over her shoulder. I shrug as I wave goodbye.

It isn't her fault she looks like her grandmother.

And as soon as she's gone, Grandma Shirley calms down. Acts like nothing happened. Tells me that we should be getting inside so she doesn't miss one of her shows.

I stay with her a long time, making sure she's OK. But she seems totally fine. Except when I try to bring up the Revelry again.

"It was a long time ago, Bitsy. Why do you keep going on about it?"

And I can't force myself to say it out loud. To ask the truth about the boy who disappeared.

Eighteen

I can't believe Amy has dragged me to the ice rink.

I hate ice skating. It makes me feel awkward and clumsy – and it is freezing. Who pays to be this cold?

But Amy has always loved it. We used to go every year for her birthday. The only reason I know how to ice skate at all is because of Amy.

The Ember Grove ice rink is in a big old barn that the Byrne family bought and converted into an ice rink of all things. It isn't fancy, just the ice and a little snack bar. It always smells like a mix of feet and frost, which are two things that definitely do not – and *should* not – go together.

Ever.

I don't want to be here. I want to be in the woods, hanging out with Skyler.

I want to be buried in a book about the town's history, or gently trying to coax Revelry secrets from the pages of the newspapers.

The only person I've told about what my grandma said is Amy, but she's more worried about my grandma's health than about "some old rumour about a boy dying". And I've been looking up as much as I can, but local journalists seem more interested in which dog has won the annual town dog show, or who is engaged than asking questions about exactly what happens at the Revelry.

And then Amy had the audacity to complain to me about how little time we're spending together, when she is the one spending all her time with Mark Lee, now that they are official. She was right, the night they hung out was different. I heard all about it. And I'm happy for her, I really am. Mark is a good guy, and Amy deserves to be with someone like him. But I'm finding it hard to care about, well, what Skyler would call silly high-school things when there is so much more to think about. But when Amy asked if I wanted to go to the ice rink, even though I hate it, I figured I should take the opportunity to spend time with her.

It will be nice to spend time with just the two of us. How things always used to be.

At least that is what I think until I look up from tying my skates and see Mark and Steve sauntering towards us.

I shoot Amy a look.

She gives me a *"Who me?"* look back and winks. "I knew if I told you I'd invited Mark and Steve, you wouldn't want to come."

"I thought you wanted to spend more time with me."

"And this *is* time with you. And time with Mark and Steve. A win-win."

I groan. "Amy, this isn't cool."

"Come on, Bits. For me?"

I sigh heavily and then stand up, wobbling on the thin blades of the skates. I plaster a smile on for Mark and Steve as they approach. They are both grinning, wearing their varsity letterman jackets and nudging each other in that way that boys do.

"I should warn you guys I'm a pretty terrible skater," I say, forcing some light-hearted cheer into my voice.

"Pretend you're swimming," says Steve with a guffaw.

I stare at him. He must be kidding. "That … doesn't make any sense."

"Yeah it does." He raises his brows incredulously, like he can't believe he has to explain this to me. "Ice *is* water. Just frozen."

"Uh-huh," I say.

"Dude – Steve – you are such an idiot," says Mark, but he's laughing. He reaches over and tugs on Amy's

174

ponytail. "You look cute." I look away, feeling like I'm intruding just by standing next to them.

"It's funny," Steve insists. "Water? Ice? If this rink melts, we're all swimming."

Amy's laughing now too and leaning into Mark, even though I know she is perfectly capable of walking on her skates. Much better than I can, at least.

I am not laughing. It is decidedly *not* funny.

"Whatever," I mutter and hobble over to the ice, leaving the three of them behind me. I hate that first step more than anything. When the ground beneath you changes. So I'm still clinging to the side of the wall when I gingerly step out.

"Hurry up, slowpoke!" says Amy cheerfully from behind me. I grit my teeth to keep from snapping at her. I move out of the way as she gracefully steps out onto the ice and begins to skate backwards.

"Comes on, Bits. Don't let your fear get the better of you."

"We'll skate with you," Mark says from behind me. He's on the ice now too, looking as confident as ever.

I manage a smile. "I'll be fine," I say. "I don't want to slow you guys down." Then, because I know it is what Amy wants, I ask where Steve is.

"Getting a hot dog. He'll be out in a minute, I'm sure."

Amy and Mark linger near me for a minute, but their hands keep brushing against each other.

There aren't that many other people here. A couple of little kids horsing around. A girl in one of those skating leotards who looks like she takes it Very Seriously.

And us.

I blow a strand of hair out of my face. "I'm going to do a lap on my own. Just to remember how to do this. I'll meet you guys back here."

"Are you sure?" says Amy.

"Yeah," I say. Because that's the response she wants to hear.

"We'll be watching to make sure you don't fall," says Mark. Then he takes Amy's hand in his own. She smiles so widely that, despite how annoyed I am at her, I can't help but smile too.

They skate off to the middle of the rink, where the ice is smoother and not as carved up as it is around the edges, where the cowards like me cling to the walls for balance.

One foot in front of the other, I tell myself. *Swish, swish.* I guess it is kind of fun. Soothing, in a way. *Swish, swish.*

There's a thump against the glass and I stumble, but catch the wall just in time.

It's Steve. He gives me a big thumbs up.

"I'll be right out," he says, his mouth full of hot dog.

"Great!" I say. And then I pick up the pace of my skating.

Swish, swish. I'm getting the hang of this, I think. I'm almost halfway across the rink. I glance up to see where Mark and Amy are. To see if they are proud of my progress.

They are standing still, in the centre of the rink, and Mark is leaning close to Amy, and his hands are on her waist and she's closing her eyes.

They're kissing. Mark and Amy are kissing in the middle of the goddamn ice rink. There are little kids here! What are they thinking?

But I know they aren't thinking at all. They are just *feeling.* All full of butterflies for each other.

And I'm jealous in a way that doesn't make sense. I don't want to be kissing either of them, and I certainly don't want to be kissing hot-dog-breath Steve, but I feel like I'm watching a snow globe that I can't get into. And I want to shake that snow globe so hard until I can't see anything but an angry flurry of snow.

With a sigh, I push off on the ice again.

And my skates slide out from under me, and I crash onto the ice.

Nineteen

My wrist hurts so much I'm scared to look at it, convinced that it is broken and bent backwards. Maybe the bone is sticking out.

Amy is there in an instant. "Bitsy! Are you all right?"

And I'm mad. I'm mad at her. It is her fault I'm here at the stupid ice rink. And, even though I know it isn't logical, I feel like if she hadn't been kissing Mark, if she'd been paying attention to me, spending time with me, I wouldn't have fallen.

I was so distracted by their PDA I fell over.

I'm still on the ice, and the cold is seeping through my jeans. I finally look at my wrist and inhale sharply through my teeth. It is bent, but it doesn't look broken. At least, there are no bones sticking out.

"Here, let me take a look." Mark is all competent kindness and I hate it. "What happened here?" he says, gingerly touching my ring scar. "Did you scrape your hand against the ice?"

On instinct, I look at Amy's hand. Her ring scar is smooth and barely visible. Not the red welt that mine is. As far as I know, her ring scar has only burned once, when my dress unravelled. But that was something that happened to me. Not to her. She always comes out on top.

And I know, I *know* this is all connected. Our scars, the Revelry, her kiss, my fall – I just don't know how.

"I'm OK," I say, but my eyes are watering.

"Bitsy, you should have been more careful," Amy says, nudging my shoulder.

"This isn't my fault! You are the whole reason I'm here. And you should have been paying more attention!"

"Bitsy, that isn't fair," says Amy. She's giving me a look that says, *Don't be crazy in front of the boy I like.*

But I don't care about that. "Yeah, you're right. It isn't fair. It isn't fair that you were making out with Mark in the middle of the ice rink, and I fell down."

"Those things aren't exactly related," says Mark, an awkward smile on his face.

"THEY ARE!" I shout.

I know I sound childish, but I don't care. I'm cold, I'm wet, my wrist is killing me, everything else hurts and all I want to do is get off this damn ice.

Amy sighs and rubs her forehead. "You know what? I'm not going to fight you about this. Let's just get you up and put some ice on your wrist."

"Looks like she's got plenty of ice out here on the rink," says Steve, who chooses this very moment to skate over. He grins at me. "Here, I'll help you up. I used to play ice hockey – I got this."

Then without warning he hoists me up by the armpits and hauls me across the ice like I'm a sack of potatoes. Just when I didn't think I could feel more humiliated.

Mark insists on driving us all. "You can't drive if you have a broken wrist," he says.

"I don't think my wrist is broken."

"Just in case," he says.

"He's just trying to be nice," Amy whispers in my ear. My wrist is throbbing, my jeans are wet and I just want to go home. So I nod and climb in the backseat of his truck.

But we don't go to my house. Mark drives us to Amy's place because Amy wants Aunt Lily to take a look at my wrist.

As I'm getting out of the car, I glance back and see that Amy is kissing Mark goodbye. I roll my eyes.

Aunt Lily isn't especially glad to see us, but then she never really is. When she realizes I'm hurt though, she goes straight into nurse mode. She gently moves my wrist one direction, and then another, watching my face for a reaction.

"It's not broken," she says after a moment. "But it is a pretty bad sprain. You'll need to wrap it. I can get something from the hospital – wait here."

And then she leaves me and Amy alone.

I explode. "What the hell, Amy?"

"You aren't actually mad at me because you sprained your wrist, are you?"

"You said we were going to hang out. And then you ambushed me with a double date with Mark and Steve! And then you were just making out with Mark in front of everyone."

Amy crosses her arms. "So that's what this is about. Me and Mark kissing."

"No! It is about you being a shitty friend."

"I don't know why you can't be happy for me." Amy turns away, but I see she's blinking back tears.

"I am happy for you," I say. "Of course I am. Mark is great. But I just feel like you've been so focused on him, and on *The Wizard of Oz*..."

"Yes, I've been focused on my own life, Bitsy. And do you know what you've been focused on? The Revelry! You're obsessed. It's starting to get weird. I'm worried about you."

"And I'm worried about what happened to us at the Revelry. For a good reason! I know you seem to be over it, but something weird happened to us that night. And I think something weird happens every Revelry. Don't you remember that just talking about a boy that went missing at her own Revelry upset my grandma so much that she forgot where – when – she was? And he wasn't the only one. There are others. Did I tell you about what I found in the library? All those teenagers who went missing like Florence Lonsdale—"

Amy holds her hand up and I go quiet, like she has some power over me. I guess she does, in a way.

"Yes, you told me. You found some old newspapers. Whatever happened to Florence Lonsdale – and whoever that boy was your grandma mentioned – which she *might* be remembering wrong, Bits. You literally just said she was in distress. Maybe something else upset her?"

I remember that it was Skyler who upset my grandma. But I can't tell Amy that because I haven't told her anything about Skyler.

Amy keeps talking. "Tragedies happened, but none of it has anything to do with us."

"I don't know why you won't listen to me." My voice cracks, and I am embarrassed by how desperate I sound, but I need Amy to understand. Somehow.

"Because you sound crazy."

That stings. I go quiet, just as Aunt Lily comes back in with a splint. She carefully sets my wrist and tells me to be more careful.

If she notices that I leave without saying bye to Amy, she doesn't mention it.

I walk through town, back to the ice rink, back to where my car is sitting alone in the parking lot.

When I get in, I slam the door, put my head on the wheel and start to cry.

I'm so mad at Amy, but it isn't just that. It is that I feel completely and utterly alone.

Twenty

The aftermath of the ice rink fiasco is that I have to wear a splint for two weeks, and Mark starts driving Amy to school in the mornings. When Amy tells me this, she's giddy, like carpooling is the modern equivalent of being whisked away on horseback.

And at lunch, they hang all over each other. Literally. She'll have her arms draped around his neck or he'll be standing behind her, holding her waist and nuzzling her neck like they are in a perpetual prom-photo pose. Mark has started taking more of an interest in my life, asking me about swimming or my family, and Amy just beams at him when he does, like he should get a gold medal for being able to hold a normal conversation. But, it's nice of them to attempt to include me in their little bubble, even if it makes me feel like more of a third wheel. And he has the decency to look a bit ashamed when I tell him I can't swim for three weeks, not until my wrist is healed.

Other than Art History, the only time I have with Amy these days is when we are on the same shift at Chanterelle's. So I'm really pleased when I see her name on the shift sheet on Friday afternoon. Less thrilled when it's twenty minutes after she was supposed to be there, and she still isn't.

"Where's your friend?" asks Chanterelle, coming in from the back and seeing me drowning in orders of herbal teas. I'm slower than I usually am because of the splint on my wrist.

I don't want Amy to get in trouble. "She's in the bathroom," I say. Chanterelle frowns, and I immediately regret the lie. She tells fortunes on the side! Of course she's going to know I'm lying. But then she simply nods and goes back to the office.

I text Amy.

Where are you? Chanterelle is asking about you!

Sorry! On my way! Rehearsal ran late.

I get back to making lattes and taking orders, tamping down my irritation.

But things keep going wrong. I drop a pot of rose tea. The toaster won't turn on. A dove flies into the café and won't leave. Stupid bird.

185

So by the time Amy bursts in through the front door, cheeks flushed, lipstick smeared, hair mussed, I'm fuming. And I know why she's late. Rehearsal didn't run long. She's been with Mark.

Just as she's joining me behind the counter, Chanterelle reappears again, looking even more disgruntled as she takes in the lengthening line and the unhappy customers.

"Sorry I'm late," says Amy. "It won't happen again."

Chanterelle looks back and forth between the two of us, and then at the line snaking towards the front door. "At the end of your shift, I'd like to speak to both of you."

A headache starts to pound behind my left temple. It's been a long day, a long week, and all I want is to go home and take a bath. I'd thought that Amy and I would get to hang out today, that maybe we could try to fix things between us, and she messed it up and she doesn't even care.

At the end of our shift, Chanterelle appears, looking sterner than I've seen her.

"Amy, you won't be late again, will you?" she says. Amy shakes her head quickly.

"Good," says Chanterelle. "Now, Bitsy, I'd like a word with you. Alone."

I frown. I haven't done anything wrong. *I* was on time.

"Of course," I say. I look at Amy.

She shrugs. "I'll call you later," she says, and then slips out of the door, already texting. Probably asking Mark for a lift. It shouldn't bother me, but it does.

"Sit down, Bitsy," says Chanterelle. As I do, I notice with rising panic that my ring scar is burning again.

And I know now what that means. Something bad is about to happen.

"Bitsy, you seem like a good girl. I hired you because your grandmother asked me to. But, I can't have someone in here who lies to me."

"I didn't lie to you," I say.

"You said your friend was in the bathroom when she wasn't. That's a lie. If you'll lie about that, who knows what else you'll lie about?"

"But she was the one who was late!"

"And she admitted it and apologized. But you seem unable to take responsibility for your actions. You lied, and I can't have a liar working in my café. So I'm going to have to let you go. I'm sorry, but I told you when you ran out the other week that was your one and only chance. You don't get a second. You might be Shirley's granddaughter, but that only goes so far. I'm sorry." She reaches out and rests her hand briefly on mine. Then she frowns. "But before you go, let me make you an oint-ment for that," she says, eyeing my ring scar. "It doesn't look like it is healing properly." She gently reaches out and rubs her thumb on my ring scar, her frown deepen-ing. It looks like she's going to ask me something else, but then she shakes her head and disappears into the back room.

When I tell my parents that night that I'm no longer working at Chanterelle's, I don't tell the whole truth.

"Working there has been fun," I say. (Lie number one.) "But I'm worried it is distracting me from school. Especially with my swim team commitments." (Lies two and three. I am distracted, but it isn't by working at Chanterelle's. And I can't swim for another week or so.)

"Oh, that's a shame," my mom says, sounding distracted as she stirs risotto on the stove. "Maybe next year you'll have more time?"

My mom believes so much in the power of being a Clark that she thinks I could walk away from a job and just … get it again next year.

I have a small twinge of guilt as I think about how easy things usually are for me. Or at least how easy they always have been until now. Amy texts to make sure I'm OK, and when I text back to tell her what happened, she calls me immediately. This is the Amy I know, the Amy who is my best friend – loyal and caring. And just as I'd hoped, she is livid on my behalf. "But that's ridiculous," she says. "You weren't lying; you were just trying to help a friend."

"I tried to tell her that," I say. "But she said if I'd lie about that, what else would I lie about?" I'm waiting for Amy to apologize, to take responsibility, to say that it was her fault, to say that if she hadn't been late, I wouldn't have lied and I wouldn't have gotten fired.

But she doesn't. She is strangely quiet, and just lets me keep talking. So I do. Waiting for her to jump in. And she stays quiet.

"The whole thing is ridiculous. I can't believe it. I mean, who does she think she is?"

Still no response from Amy.

"You're obviously going to quit, right? I mean, you wouldn't have got this job without me. It was a favour for my grandma. It's not fair if you stay on after I got fired. Especially since I got fired because of you."

Amy still doesn't say anything. I wonder if the line has cut out. "Did you hear me? I said I got fired because of you."

Amy makes a derisive snort. Apparently the line hasn't cut out. "You lied to our boss and got fired. And you think that is my fault. You are actually blaming me." She snorts again. "Bitsy, that's ridiculous. Even for you."

"What is *that* supposed to mean? Even for me?"

"Bits, we all know that you have trouble taking responsibility for things. Remember when you blamed me for falling on the ice? It isn't my fault that you are a terrible ice skater."

"It was your fault I was there in the first place! And it is your fault that you were late today and I had to lie for you."

"I never asked you to lie for me."

"That is what good friends do."

"OK, Saint Bitsy."

Her mocking tone is too much.

"If it was the other way around, I would quit in solidarity. It's the least I could do! And I'm sorry for expecting you to do the same thing."

"I'm not quitting. I need this job. And if you were such a good friend, you would know that."

And with that, she hangs up.

Twenty-one

I'm furious at Amy, but not as furious as I am at myself. I toss and turn all night, getting more and more upset. The next morning, I have dark circles under my eyes and two new pimples.

And my ring scar is still stinging.

So when Grandma Shirley asks me to come help her in her garden, it feels like the perfect distraction. Even though I don't really want to be digging weeds up all day, I do want to spend time with her. And I know if I stay holed up in my room feeding on nothing but my own anger and frustration, I'll just feel worse.

Of course the first thing she asks me about is how things are going at Chanterelle's.

"I hope my friend is treating you well," she says, pulling on her gardening gloves. "She and I have quite the history."

"She fired me yesterday," I say.

"What?" My grandma whips her head up so fast I'm worried she might hurt herself. "On what grounds?"

And however high and mighty I'd felt, now that I have to spell it out for my grandma, I realize that maybe ... maybe I might deserve it. I might not have told my parents the truth, but I'm not going to lie to Grandma Shirley.

"And Amy isn't on my side at all," I finish.

Grandma Shirley shakes her head and tuts. At first I think she's tutting about Amy. But then she speaks. "Bitsy, you know things haven't been easy for Amy. She's only got her Aunt Lily to care for her. Her mother died when she was so young. And her father, well he's been away a long time now, hasn't he?"

"What does that have to do with her not being on my side about this?" I grumble.

"Well it is like she said: she needs this job more than you do. You should think about where she's coming from."

I snip at a thorny stem. "I feel like I'm always putting her first. That I'd do anything for her. But it doesn't always feel reciprocated. I go to all her shows, I let her wear my clothes, I ask about her and Mark, I got her a job, covered for her..."

"My dear little goose, have you ever thought that sometimes people see friendship differently? Perhaps the way you think a good friend should act is different to what Amy thinks. There isn't a rule book on friendship. Each of us can only do the best we can, and hope that the other is doing the same."

"So you don't think she should have quit?" I say.

"You aren't going to like my answer," my grandma says, with a small smile.

"So you think it is fine for her to stay on, even though she is the reason I got fired."

Grandma Shirley puts down her gardening shears and trundles over to me, rubbing my back. "I think we are going to need a stronger tonic than gardening to help with this one. Let's make peanut butter chocolate cookies. Those always cheer you up."

"I'm not five," I say, but I can't hold back my grin. "You can't magically fix everything with my favourite cookies."

"Maybe not, but they can't hurt. And, my dearest, it isn't Amy's fault that you were fired. She shouldn't have been late, but she didn't ask you to lie for her. I'm sorry Chanterelle fired you, I really am. But it isn't the end of the world. It's an after-school job. And you don't need it the way Amy does. It will be OK. Most things are, in the end."

My stomach growls and she grins.

"Come on, let's go make those cookies."

She's right, of course: the cookies do make me feel better. The whole act of mixing the dough (and eating some of it straight from the mixing bowl), shaping the cookies, breathing in their fresh-baked cookie smell when they come out of the oven, and then picking out the perfect ones to eat first, it is like some sort of small magic. I know Amy loves these too, so I take a picture and text it to her.

Baked with Grandma Shirley today. Saved you some. I'll bring them on Monday. xo

I'm worried she might not reply, but less than five minutes later my phone pings.

Yum! Give her a hug from me. And thanks for saving me some. xo

"What are you smiling at your phone for? It's not a person, you do know that, right?" says Grandma Shirley as she bustles around me, reaching for another peanut butter chocolate cookie. I put my phone on silent, and follow her into the living room to make a jigsaw puzzle.

On Monday, when I pull into the parking lot, Amy untangles herself from Mark and comes and knocks on my car window.

I roll it down.

"Can I come in?" she asks, and I nod.

I hand her a plastic container full of peanut butter chocolate cookies. She bites into one and closes her eyes.

"These are so damn good," she says. Then she looks at me. "Thanks for saving me some."

"I wouldn't deny you Grandma Shirley's peanut butter chocolate cookies just because we're fighting. That would be an atrocity."

"You know I hate it when we fight," says Amy, taking another bite of cookie. "I missed you over the weekend."

I snort. "Liar. You were with Mark all weekend. I bet you barely even thought about me."

"I did! Honest! And I told Mark about our fight — I hope that's OK — and he helped make me realize that I could have been a little more understanding. And nicer."

Ten points for Mark Lee, I think. And I mean it. I appreciate that he's on my side here.

"You aren't mad that I told him, are you?"

"Of course not. He's your boyfriend. I expect you to tell him things. I mean, so long as it's not, like, secret things."

"Never," says Amy. "Are you still mad at me for not quitting?" She reaches out and squeezes my hand.

I look at our linked hands, our matching ring scars.

I shake my head. "I get it," I say. And I do. I know she needs this job. "And I'm sorry for not thinking about how the job might be different for each of us. I didn't realize how self-centred I was being." I squeeze back.

"Thanks," she says. "That means a lot. And for the record, I'm still pissed at Chanterelle for firing you. Not that I'll tell her that, of course. I feel like she could turn me into a toad if she wanted."

I laugh. "I guess I got off lucky just getting fired." Then I glance out of the window at Mark. "Now that we're officially not fighting … want to tell me about your weekend with Mark?"

"Well, we're officially going to homecoming together," she says. And then she tells me all the details about how he asked her. Dinner and dessert, with *"Homecoming?"* spelled out on a plate in chocolate. I *ooh* and *ah*, even as I feel a tight punch of envy right in my stomach. And then she tells me that Steve is going to ask me.

I close my eyes, trying to tamp down my frustration. "Amy, you remember what happened the last time the four of us got together. I almost broke my wrist."

"This is totally different," she says with a laugh. "Dancing is way less lethal than ice-skating."

And I know this is Amy trying to be nice, trying to include me, but I hate that she did this, orchestrated who would take me to homecoming without even asking me. She's just thinking of what would be best for her.

And a small part of me wonders if she thinks that I can't get a date for the dance on my own. That I need her to intervene. That without her, nobody would want me.

I don't know what I'm expecting from Steve, but it isn't a paper aeroplane thrown at my head in Art History with *"BB – Homecoming? Should be dope. Steve"* on it.

I'm definitely not expecting Mr de Freston to see said aeroplane hit my head, and open it up and read the note to the whole class. Amy squeals in delight when she hears it, like this is all a good thing. Like BB doesn't stand for 'Big Bits' – a name she knows I hate.

"So don't leave us in suspense, Bitsy," Mr de Freston says dryly. "What's the answer?"

I can barely make eye contact with Steve, but I don't want to embarrass him or myself any further, so I smile and nod. "Of course," I say.

"Sweet," Steve replies.

"Sweet indeed," says Mr de Freston. "Now back to the topic at hand: who can identify the painting on the screen, and explain why it broke tradition with other paintings of the French Renaissance?"

Of course Steve has asked me only five days before the dance. With barely any time left to find a dress. But Amy takes it as a challenge, and so two days before the dance itself, we go dress shopping at the second-hand shop. I might not care about the dance – and I definitely don't care about Steve – but I still want to look nice. I like looking back at my mom's old pictures and if I ever have a daughter, I want to show her what I looked like when I was young and going to school dances.

We're at the back of the shop when Amy finds the most gorgeous silver dress for me. At first I think she wants it for herself, but then she holds it out. "This dress was made for you, Bits."

I shake my head. It is way too skimpy for my figure.

"Just trust me," she says.

And when I try it on and look in the mirror, I gasp. It is the most beautiful thing I've ever worn. It's silver and silky and looks like it is made of melted starlight.

When I buy it, the shop owner gives it a wistful look. "Oh, that is one of my favourites," she says. And I want to ask about the story, where it came from. Maybe it went to a Revelry. But then Amy is there, buying her dress, and the moment has passed.

I go to the woods a few times, looking for Skyler, but there's no sign of her. I hope she remembers our plan for homecoming. Just because I have a date now, doesn't mean that I'm not more excited about meeting up with her in the woods. And then it's Friday, the day of the dance. I try to be excited, for Amy's sake. But all I can think about is what Skyler has planned for when we meet up.

"You are going to look amazing!" Amy trills as she ties the back of my dress up. She's lined my eyes in silver and black, and painted my lips cherry red. She puts more curls in my hair, and it all cascades down my back. Amy is wearing a vintage black-and-white polka-dot dress with roses on it, and looks incredible. When Mark and Steve come to my house to pick us up, the expression on Mark's face when he sees her sends a strange kind of longing into my stomach. It isn't jealousy, exactly, because I don't want Mark looking at me like that – I want him looking at Amy like that – but I want someone to look at me like that. The look that I do get, from Steve, is a once-over, lingering far too long on my boobs, and then a thumbs up. "Looking good, Big Bits."

What every girl wants to hear from their homecoming date.

When we get to the dance, it's clear that Steve has no intention of spending any time with me. He disappears

199

into the bathroom for a suspiciously long time, and returns reeking of booze. He half-heartedly dances with me for a song or two, and then spends the rest of the night bouncing from one girl in our group to the next.

And even though I didn't want to go with him in the first place, it stings. It stings that I'm clearly not his first choice of a dance date (although it is unclear who was), and it stings that he apparently needs to be wasted to get through an evening of being my date (even though he's not even spending any time with me). And what stings the most is that, throughout all of this, Amy, who said the whole reason she wanted me to go with Steve is so we could all have fun at the dance *together*, hasn't even noticed. She's spent the whole night making out and dancing with Mark. I thought that we'd be dancing together in a big group, but instead I spend most of the night awkwardly shuffling by myself until I can't stand it any more.

Amy is pretty shocked when I tap her on the shoulder and tell her I'm leaving.

"What?" she shouts above the music, pulling away from Mark. "Did you just say you're *leaving*? Come on! You have to stay." She reaches for my hands and tries to pull me towards her to dance. "The night is just getting started! Let's dance!"

And that is the last straw for me.

"Don't pretend you even notice if I'm here or not," I shout back as I rip my hands out of hers. Her eyes widen and we stare at each other for a long moment, music pulsing all around us. Then I grab Steve's suit jacket from the pile of coats in the corner (the least he can do is let me take his jacket) and march outside.

But Amy follows me out into the school parking lot. It's cold and dark, and a lone streetlight flickers on and off. Amy's heels click, the sound suddenly loud in the quiet.

"What the hell, Bitsy?"

I take a deep breath. I wish she hadn't followed me out here. I just want to leave. But she *has* come out here, and not to apologize, or make sure that I am OK, but to get mad at me … my anger bubbles over and I whirl toward her.

"I should be saying that to you! You are only happy if I'm doing exactly what YOU want, like some sort of Barbie doll you can dress up and drag around wherever you want. Well, you know what? I'm DONE doing that. I'm DONE being a side character on the Amy Show."

Amy staggers back, like I've physically struck her. But I'm just getting started.

"We always do what you want to do. Talk about what you want to talk about. You didn't even know that I wasn't swimming varsity this year."

"It isn't my fault you didn't tell me! I'm not a mind-reader."

"People who ask questions about other people's lives aren't required to read minds."

"Since when do I have to ask you about what is happening in your life? When did you stop telling me?"

"When you made it clear that you never want to listen!"

Amy stamps her foot and throws her hands up in the air. "Because all you want to talk about is a bunch of Revelry conspiracy theories."

"The whole reason we went to the Revelry is because you wanted to." I poke my finger at her chest, and immediately feel like a toddler throwing a tantrum. I'm so embarrassed that it makes tears come to my eyes. "Don't pretend you care if I'm here at the dance or not. You won't even notice when I'm gone."

"You know what, Bitsy? I will notice. I'll notice because I won't have to worry about you. To make sure that you're having fun, make sure people are including you."

I gasp. "Those are MY friends you are talking about. You wouldn't know them if it wasn't for me."

"Bitsy, get over yourself!" Amy pauses and glares at me before continuing. "Yes, you knew some of these people before I did. When you were, like, eight! Big deal. Just because I wasn't born at Ember Grove Hospital doesn't mean I don't belong here."

I narrow my eyes at her. "You don't though. Not the way that I do." As soon as the words are out, my stomach drops. I know I've gone too far. I should have never said it. Not out loud.

Amy steps back and stares at me. Then she shakes her head and scoffs. "You can be a real bitch sometimes, you know that?"

In all of our years of friendship and fights, Amy's never said anything like that to me. I swallow hard, trying to keep from crying. "Just go back inside. I have nothing to say to you."

And before I can change my mind, before she can say something else, I turn and run.

Twenty-two

I run all the way to the woods.

And tonight, I find the living room right away.

Skyler is standing in the middle of it wearing an emerald-green ballgown. It looks even more vintage than mine or Amy's. Her hair is piled on top of her head in an elaborate bun. She twirls, grinning at me. "Ta-da!"

I laugh, but I feel underdressed in my slinky silver dress. And cold.

"Your dress is incredible." I say. "Where did you get it?"

"It belonged to my grandma," she says. I wish Grandma Shirley had dresses like that lying around for me to wear. "I like your dress too. You look like you belong in the forest, like you could make the flowers bloom at midnight."

I beam at her, soaking up the praise. "Is that the plan for the evening?"

"Oh, don't you worry. I've got grand plans for us tonight. Come on!" She picks up her skirts and runs deeper into the forest. I kick off my silver heels, leaving them by the couch, and run after her.

Thorns and twigs scrape at my bare legs and feet.

I don't mind. It's the woods saying hello, nipping at my heels, urging me onwards.

And then we're at Lake Lost.

Lake Lost, glistening in the moonlight like a sheet of black glass.

For a strange moment I think I see flames flickering across the top, *flames dancing on the water*, but then all is still. A trick of the light.

I'm breathing heavily from running through the woods. Skyler seems barely out of breath.

"Well, obviously we're going to get in," she says with a mischievous smile.

"But … your dress! And your hair! And … my dress! And my hair!"

But that isn't my real worry. I don't want to admit to Skyler that I'm scared. Not just of the dark water, but that what if what goes in … doesn't come out? What if it gets lost with the lake?

"Dresses dry, darling. So does hair. Nothing but window dressing. Live a little." And with that, Skyler steps into the lake. The gown billows out around her. She looks over her shoulder at me. "Are you coming or what?"

And so I follow. I leave my suit jacket (OK, *Steve's* suit jacket) on the bank and I step into the lake, slowly at first, and then I dive under all of a sudden, the splash echoing in the quiet. When I come back up, Skyler splashes me.

"Race you across? You said you're a swimmer, didn't you?"

"Across?"

I've never thought of Lake Lost having an across. I've only ever seen it from this side of the woods.

I gaze out into the darkness. Trying to see the edge of the lake. I know it's there, but I can't see it.

I shiver in the water, and it isn't from the cold.

"I do enough racing with swim team," I say lightly.

My silver dress clings to me like a second skin, and I turn over on my back, floating, and it ripples out around me.

I float without effort. Strangely Skyler does too, despite her heavy, old-fashioned dress. I stare up at the stars. It's nice, being able to see so many. In the woods, where the trees are so dense, it's harder to see them. I'd almost forgotten they were there.

"So tell me about the dance," says Skyler. "Was it everything high-school dreams are made of?"

I snort. "Hardly."

"Allow me to let you in on a little secret, as someone older and wiser: humans will almost always let you down."

My gaze slides from the stars over to her. "Says a human."

Her mouth quirks. "I'm a special human. Rules don't apply." I laugh, but the water temperature feels like it has suddenly dropped. Then Skyler flips over so she's paddling, and tugs my hand so I'm facing her. "You're a special human too, you know that? It seems like maybe you don't know that."

I'm glad it's dark so she can't see me blush. "I'm just ... Bitsy Clark," I say. "I'm a good swimmer but that's about all I've got going for me."

"No." She shakes her head vehemently. "You can't believe that. You are brave and bold. I know that. I see it in you." Her voice drops to a whisper. "The woods see it in you."

And there, with the stars shining down on us, and the woods all around, with this strange silver-haired, mirror-eyed girl staring so intently at me, I believe it.

"If you say so," I say.

"I know so. And you know so too. It's important, Bitsy – it's important to believe it. Believing something has real power." Her eyes are shining.

Then she lets go of my hands and splashes me again. "I told you we'd do something spectacular tonight. And is this spectacular or what?"

"Yeah, it is." I grin at her.

We swim and talk and laugh for hours. Until the sky is lightening above us.

"I don't want to get out," I sigh. "It is going to be so cold. My only option is to stay in the lake forever. I'll turn into a mermaid eventually, right? That's just science."

"A lake mermaid? Where's the fun in that? Surely if you're going to turn into a mermaid, you'd want it to be in the ocean. You'd get bored in here after about a day."

I sigh again, dramatically. "I guess you're right. You know, I've never actually seen the ocean."

"Me neither," says Skyler. "Maybe one day."

"We aren't that far. My brother goes to Cobalt, down on the coast. It is only a few hours away."

"Might as well be another planet," Skyler mutters.

"What?" I don't get it.

"It's just ... sometimes anything outside of Ember Grove seems so far away, you know?"

I do know. I nod emphatically. "But you've graduated now," I say encouragingly. "You can go anywhere."

My words echo in the dark.

I know that not everyone gets to leave Ember Grove. And this year, it seems Skyler is the only one left behind.

"Anywhere," Skyler repeats dreamily. Then she turns and splashes me. "Come on, let's get back to shore."

We swim back to the edge of the lake. I pull on Steve's jacket, grateful to have it. Skyler's dress is soaking, but she doesn't seem to mind.

"That was fun," she says, her eyes still bright. Then she reaches out and places her hand gently on my cheek. "I wanted to show you something fun."

"Well, you succeeded."

"Oh, Bitsy Clark. I'm glad you snuck into the Revelry." She begins to hum, that song that haunts me in my dreams.

"What is that?" I say, but she just smiles and keeps humming.

The sound makes me dizzy.

And then we're back at the living room. Or I am. Skyler is gone. And I'm suddenly so tired. All the dancing and the swimming. It is all catching up with me. The couch looks so comfortable. I'll lie down for just a moment. These are my woods. I'm safe here.

Twenty-three

Amy is screaming my name.

I jolt upright, heart pounding, palms sweaty.

The air around me is silent and still.

It was a dream. I shake my head, shaking the dream memory out. It sounded so real. My ring scar is burning. But that's nothing new. I rub it absent-mindedly.

Skyler is still gone. I try to remember what happened after Lake Lost, but it is all a little fuzzy. I was so tired. I'm glad I got some rest.

I glance at my phone. Almost nine in the morning. I should get home.

When I emerge out of the trees and back into the real world, my phone starts buzzing with unread texts. Buzzing and buzzing.

And buzzing.

They are all from Amy.

23.17: I'm sorry.

23.34: I don't understand what happened. Why were you so mad?

23.46: Bits, even if you are mad, you can reply. This is bullshit.

23.55: Hellooo?

00.16: Bitsy, where are you?

00.32: The dance is over and everyone is going back to Steve's house, but I want to find you. I'm coming to find you. We don't lose each other, remember? No matter what.

01.04: I've turned on find my friends and it looks like you are somewhere in the woods. Why would you go into the woods in the middle of the night?

02.14: Bits, my scar, the one from that night, it hurts. I'm scared something bad is happening. Please answer me. It's been hours.

02.45: Where are you? This isn't funny any more.

03.30: I'm going into the woods. I'm going to find you.

Chills skitter all over my body. Surely she must have gone home and fallen asleep. I don't bother texting, but call right away.

It rings and rings and rings. No answer.

I text her.

Amy, I'm OK! Where are you?

The message doesn't even go through.

Damn it.

I scroll through my phone. There it is. Mark Lee's number. I call and it rings and rings, then goes to voicemail. I hang up and text him. He has to know where she is.

Shit.

I'm on the street now and the way I see it, I have two choices.

I can go home, shower, change and go look for Amy.

Or I can go looking for her right now. The nearest house is the Gordons'. And in the front yard, just like I knew there would be, are three bikes laying in a heap, wet with dew. I grab the biggest one, the one that belongs to ten-year-old Gabbie, and hop on it.

I text my mom.

Grabbing breakfast with everyone. Back later.

Not a lie, more of a prediction. Hopefully.

I bike as fast as I can to Steve's house. The suit jacket flies out behind me and my dress is hiked up around my thighs but I don't care who sees me. All I care about is finding Amy.

212

Steve lives just two streets down, so I'm at his house in just a few minutes. I knock on his door as loud as I can and then lean on the doorbell. Again and again and again.

There is a scuffle behind the door and then it is yanked open.

Steve is in his boxers, his hair sticking up everywhere, and he stares at me in confusion.

"Jesus, Bitsy, where's the fire?"

"Is Amy here?" I demand, pushing past him, like maybe she's hiding right behind him in the kitchen.

"Amy? No, she went looking for you." He squints. "Is that my jacket?"

I ignore that. "Is Mark here?"

"Um, yeah, I'll get him."

But Mark has already come down the stairs, in sweatpants and no shirt, eyes wide with a growing panic. The same panic that is bubbling beneath my skin.

"Amy's not with you?" he says.

And I swear my heart fully stops before thumping to life in double time. My ring scar is a livid, angry welt across my finger. I rub it with my thumb.

"No," I say. And then I swallow. "I think she's in the woods."

Mark insists we go to Aunt Lily's apartment first, even though I know, *I know I know I know,* in my heart and in my veins that Amy won't be there. I gaze up at the old hospital. I'm not afraid of it tonight. I feel like I could face anything if it means finding Amy.

We ring the buzzer, but as I predicted, nobody is home. Not even Aunt Lily. She must still be on a shift at the hospital. But I have a key to the apartment, hanging on my key ring next to my own house keys. It doesn't take long to go through each room and confirm that the apartment is indeed empty. I haven't been here since the night of the Revelry, and I'd forgotten how small it is.

"She went looking for you," Mark says, voice heavy with accusation. I flinch, like he's thrown the words at me.

"You should have gone with her," I say. "You're from here. You know the woods. Amy doesn't know the woods. Not like you and I do."

"She didn't tell me she was going to the woods! She said she was going to your house!" Mark says. Then, "What are you doing?"

I'm rifling through her closet. "Looking for something to wear," I say, gesturing at the still-damp silver dress. "Something I can move around in better than this." I grab a pair of leggings and a sweatshirt. "I'll meet you back in your car."

When I'm alone in Amy's room, I close my eyes and breathe in slowly. Like if I try hard enough I'll be able to smell her, and find her.

My ring scar is burning like it never has before.

We won't lose each other, I tell myself. *We can't.*

By the time we get to the woods, the sky has opened up above us. It starts as a drizzle, but as we search, the rain grows heavier and heavier. Hours go by, the mud getting thicker beneath our feet, slowing us down as we slog through the woods, calling Amy's name. We don't even stop for lunch, and by the time the sun starts to set, we're both sopping wet. Still no sign of Amy.

I trace and retrace my own steps, like somehow that will lead me to her.

Not only do I not find Amy, I can't find the living room, or Lake Lost, or any sign of Skyler. The trees are different from those I walked through this morning. I should have come back then, on my own.

Now it's like doors are slamming in my face at every turn. Mark and I go in circles, coming back to the same trees and the same rocks and the same glens over and over and over again no matter how many different trails we take. He's getting jumpier by the minute and I don't blame him.

"She'll be OK," I say, as if by saying it I'll believe it too.

I know she is OK: I can feel it. I'd know if something really bad had happened to her.

"She'll be OK," I repeat, shouting to Mark over the pounding of the rain. The drops are hitting the ground so hard it is difficult to hear. "She'll find shelter." *Get warm, get safe*, I think, and I press my ring scar with my thumb. *I'll find you. We're coming.*

We stumble out of the forest, and are at the back of Chanterelle's. She's in the garden, planting something, and hurries over to us. "What are you two doing out in this weather? Come in and get warm."

Once we are inside she says, "Bitsy, it's good to see you, but, my dear, you are positively drenched." She eyes Mark. "I've seen you before, haven't I?"

"This is Amy's boyfriend," I say. "We're looking for Amy. Nobody can find her. Has she been here?"

Chanterelle pales. A girl gone missing in Ember Grove is no good thing. "When did you last see her?" she asks, sitting down with us. She calls to Tony, asks for fresh hot water and tea leaves, and I know she's going to try to see where Amy is.

I'm strangely comforted.

She drinks her tea down and then studies the leaves. Her eyes glaze over for a moment and then she snaps her

216

head up. "She's still in the woods. And she can't get out on her own. You must find her before it gets too late."

We know we have to tell Aunt Lily and my parents.

I have Aunt Lily's number in my phone. She answers, but I can tell that she is trying to convince herself that it isn't a big deal, that teen girls run off sometimes.

"She's lost," I say. "She didn't run off. I think we should call the police."

"Her mom was like this," Aunt Lily says. "Always causing drama. Expecting me to clean up after her messes. Amy will come home when she is ready to."

My heart is rent in two at such callous words.

I call my mom next, who has already sent me four anxious texts wondering where I am since last she heard from me is that I was going to breakfast, and she's more concerned than Aunt Lily, especially when I tell her I think Amy is in the woods. "Don't go looking for her on your own," my mom says, and I almost let out a wild laugh at how little she knows me. She still thinks I'm Good Girl Bitsy who would never go in the woods by herself. Haven't they noticed? Haven't they seen? Of course not.

I wonder what she would do if she knew how often I frequent the woods these days. Or more accurately, these nights. I know the woods and the woods know me, I want to tell her. But I don't. I pretend to be the Good Girl Bitsy she thinks I am.

Mark calls his mom too, and I can tell by his frown and the way he runs his hand through his hair that she's worried.

"My mom says we should go to the police. She can't come with us right now, she's closing up at the bakery, but she says that is what we should do. And I agree. Especially if Amy's aunt isn't going to do anything."

So we go to the Ember Grove police station. I feel like we're pretending. Like we should have an adult with us. We're covered in mud and have leaves in our hair: who is going to take us seriously? But at least the police woman listens. Until she hears where we think Amy is, and then she holds her hands up. "You know the woods are not within our jurisdiction," she says, and I can tell she feels bad. "We'll send someone out there to help look for her, but…" Her voice trails off.

"I know," I say. We all know there's no policing the woods.

I haven't told Aunt Lily or my parents or anyone the full truth. That Amy went in the woods looking for me. That it is my fault. Only Mark knows that. And he keeps glaring at me, but he doesn't say anything.

I have to find her.

Twenty-four

I have not been afraid of the woods since the night of the Revelry.

Tonight I am afraid.

But still, I go alone. Mark went home after we went to the police station, in case Amy looks for him there. We both swore we'd call if we heard anything. And we made plans to keep looking in the morning. But I'm not waiting until then. So as soon as I can, as soon as I'm sure my parents are asleep, I sneak out.

I can sense that I need to do this on my own. That the woods, our woods, my woods, will open for me and me alone.

Already, I see a path that Mark and I missed. A path that calls to me like a flower to a bee. I hurry down it, the flashlight on my phone turned on.

I don't trust my feet tonight. And I don't trust the trees. But I trust my heart to lead me to Amy. I press my ring scar and whisper, *where are you where are you where are you?*

The path winds through the trees, and when the air changes and smells slightly different, I know I'm close to Lake Lost.

Where Skyler and I were just last night.

I feel like I'm playing a game of hot and cold, like Harvey and I used to do when I was little. He'd hide something in the house and say, "Warmer, warmer, hot, hot, burning hot!" as I got closer, or, "Getting cooler, colder, cold, freezing cold," as I got further away. She's close. She's close.

I know that she must have looked for me the same way last night. She must have missed me at the lake. And then got lost.

She doesn't know the woods like I do.

And it is easy to get confused.

"Amy?" I call out.

Nothing.

But she's close, I'm sure of it. *Where are you where are you where are you?*

Then I see it.

A huge tree stands like a sentry in the woods, the other

trees giving it space. I remember that tree. Amy and I sat in the hollow of that tree the night of the Revelry. A tree with the perfect spot for us to rest, like someone had carved it out with a spoon. I break into a run.

Around the other side of the tree, in the scooped-out hollow, is Amy.

She is curled up on her side, still in her dress from the dance. Her skin is pale and covered in dirt, her eyes are closed, and I don't think she is breathing. And in that moment, my own breath stops as well.

But then her chest rises and falls and I fly to her.

"Amy!"

She sits up with a gasp and scuttles back against the tree, eyes wide with panic.

"Amy, it's me," I say, kneeling in the dirt and reaching towards her. "It's Bitsy!"

Amy blinks and then falls into my arms and starts to sob. "I've been looking for you," she says. "I couldn't find you anywhere. We aren't supposed to lose each other."

"Hey, hey, it's OK," I say, hugging her. "I found you. I'm OK; you're OK. Everything is OK."

She takes a deep, shuddering breath.

"I found the tree," she says, sniffling. "I remembered it from the Revelry. I was so tired, I felt like I'd been walking forever and I thought maybe I'd find you at the lake but," she pauses and looks out between the trees, where the lake shines in the dark, "there was nobody there."

How is that possible? Why didn't she see me? See Skyler? Why didn't we see her? We were here all night.

But Amy's still talking, telling me what happened. "And then I couldn't find my way back home, so I came back here to rest."

"That was smart," I murmur as soothingly as I can. "And we're going to go home now." I get to my feet and pull Amy up with me. "Let's go."

I text Aunt Lily and Mark, and put a call through to the police officer on the number she gave me. My parents are sleeping. The house is breathing softly the way it does at night, I imagine in rhythm with my parents.

I give Amy water and some cake that Grandma Shirley baked. I can tell from the way she keeps looking up at me, a bit like a wounded animal, that she's mad at me but isn't ready to talk about it.

I'm mad at her too. But I don't say that. And I'm more relieved than anything. But still, underneath the relief is a hot anger. Why did she come looking for me? I was fine. She was the one who got lost in the woods, not me.

But I don't say that. Instead I give her more cake. Amy showers and then changes into a pair of my pyjamas and we curl up, like we have so many times before, next to each other in my bed. Right before she falls asleep, Amy grabs my hand. "Thank you for finding me," she murmurs, and then she falls asleep, her head flopping onto my shoulder.

It takes me longer to fall asleep, and the last thing I notice before I do is that my ring scar doesn't hurt any more.

Twenty-five

I tell my parents that Amy showed up in the night outside the house.

They accept this, even though I see my mom's eyes slide over both of us, like she can read the scratches on our legs and the lies in our eyes.

Amy isn't ready to go home to Aunt Lily, and I don't blame her. I remember how harsh Aunt Lily sounded when we told her Amy was missing.

My parents have to drive to another orchard in the next town, so Amy and I have the house to ourselves. We sit for a while in the silence, eating cake for breakfast.

It is only then that Amy turns to me, eyes angry, the hurt radiating off her like a fever. "Where were you?" Amy demands. "And who were you with?"

"I fell asleep in the woods."

"Bitsy. Stop lying. I know you are up to something. I went looking for you because I was worried. And we never fight the way we did outside the dance. I wanted to find you so I could say sorry. The least you could do is be honest with me."

"No, the least I could do was *actually* find you, which I did," I say, and then get up and stalk across the kitchen to make a cup of tea. "You shouldn't have gone into the woods without me," I say quietly, but not quietly enough.

"What?" Amy stands up.

"I said you shouldn't have gone into the woods without me. That is why you got lost."

"I got lost because I was looking for you! After you stormed off."

"I stormed off because you called me a bitch."

"Oh, don't pretend you weren't already leaving by then. That you weren't meeting someone. You are keeping secrets from me. And now weird things are happening."

I nearly drop my mug. "Weird things have been happening ever since the Revelry! I kept trying to tell you, but you wouldn't listen. Not until something weird happened to you."

"Fine. You're right. Weird things are happening," she says, holding out her hand. Her scar is flat but red. "My scar started to burn after you left the dance. That's why

I went looking for you. I thought something bad was happening to you. Like when your dress unravelled."

I slowly shake my head. "Maybe that's how it started, but the scars have changed – we've changed. I think … I think it must have burned because something bad was going to happen to you. And it did. You got lost in the woods. You shouldn't have gone into the woods alone. You know better than that."

"But you can?" Amy counters. She's braced herself against the kitchen table, like it is the only thing keeping her tethered, like she'd float away otherwise.

"I wasn't alone," I say. And then, all at once, I'm tired of keeping things from her.

So I tell her everything. About Skyler. About meeting in the woods.

Amy's mouth is in a thin, flat line, like a worm crawling across her face.

"So let me get this straight," she says. "While I was going round in circles in the woods, looking for you, worried about you, you were just hanging out with some random girl who lives in the woods… That isn't like you, Bitsy."

"Oh, because something interesting and exciting could never happen to me?"

"What are you talking about?" she says, and she looks

genuinely confused. "All I mean is that the Bitsy I know wouldn't disappear into the woods with someone she doesn't know."

"You think you know me so well," I say, and the venom in my voice surprises us both. "But you don't. Not really. You only know me as the Bitsy who always cheers you on. Who is there to support you. You don't care about me. You only care about having a captive audience, and I've been that for years."

Amy snaps back, eyes wide, like she's been slapped. But I don't stop.

"Skyler knows me. She thinks I'm going places. Going to do amazing things."

"How can you say that? Like I don't want the same for you! I think that too. And I don't want to fight! I went looking for you. Why can't you ever see how much I care about you?" Amy's voice is getting louder and louder as she gets more and more agitated.

"Because I always do more!" I say. "I always do more for you!"

"That isn't true," she says, her voice cracking. "And even if it was, friendship shouldn't be about keeping score."

"Easy for you to say when you always come out on top."

Amy's nose is getting red, which I know means she's about to cry. I should stop, but I don't.

"And stop giving yourself so much credit for looking for me. I went looking for you too, you know? And I found you!" I lift my hand up – half to stop her, half to show her. "My scar burned too. Because the bad thing happening to you was also bad for me. Because I care more. But all the times my scar has burned before, all the bad things that have been happening to me, you haven't noticed. Has your scar even burned other than that one time when my dress unravelled?"

I glare at her and she looks down at her hand and says, "Maybe it is just a scar. Maybe I scraped it on something last night. It doesn't mean anything."

"Exactly. Your scar is just a scar. Everything is going great for you. More than great. You've been getting everything you want!"

And as I say it, I realize how true it is. I replay everything that has happened between me and Amy since the Revelry. All the good things that have happened to her. All the bad things that have happened to me.

Like when I was fired. Because of her.

I think about how she wouldn't quit Chanterelle's, even though I would have quit for her.

I feel like I've been giving, and giving, and giving, and she's just been taking, and taking, and taking.

She looks like I've smacked her. I guess I have in a way.

"I don't know what you want from me," she says, and her voice is wobbling and I don't want to hurt my best friend but I don't know how to make this stop, how to change things so that things even out.

"I just want you to believe me," I say. "Something weird is happening to us and it's hurting me more than it hurts you."

We stare at each other in silence for a long moment. Amy speaks first. "I already told you I believed you, Bitsy."

"OK. Thank you."

"Thank you for coming to find me," she says, and her voice is hoarse now, like she's all worn out.

"I wouldn't have had to if you hadn't come to find me," I say, and give her a tentative smile.

"Bits, what do you mean, your ring scar burns all the time?" she says, reaching for my hand to inspect my scar.

The doorbell rings, startling us both before I can respond.

It's Mark Lee.

The second he sees her, he takes Amy in his arms and she curls up against his chest and he holds her as she cries. "You're safe," he says.

Like she wasn't until he got here. Even though I'm the one who found her.

But then, I guess it is sort of my fault she was in the woods in the first place.

We are in *my* kitchen, and I feel like I'm the one intruding.

It is an icky feeling.

But then Mark speaks up again. "I'm so glad you found our Ames," he says, and his dark eyes are kind and warm. He starts to laugh a little, the low sound echoing in the kitchen like a familiar song. "Ames, Bitsy showed up at Steve's house at the crack of dawn on a bike, wearing a suit jacket over her dress – it was wild. You should have seen her. She was like some kind of warrior, and she was going to find you come hell or high water."

"Sounds like Bitsy," says Amy, giving me a grin.

I wonder if Amy has told him anything about the Revelry. Or if she's at least tried. I think of how every time I've tried to talk about it to anyone the words got stuck in my throat. It's not like *anyone* round here ever talks about it. Maybe the whole damn thing has always been cursed.

"Have you seen your aunt yet?" Mark asks Amy.

She shakes her head. "I should … I should probably get home," she says.

"I'll drive you," he says, moving closer to her like he can protect her from what happened in the woods.

I'm suddenly exhausted. I wish someone was trying to protect me. But I'm not mad at Amy for having Mark. I'm not mad at her at all now. I just want things to go back to how they used to be. She came looking for me, and that means something. It means a lot.

"Should have known you would find her," says Mark, punching me affectionately on the shoulder. "Never doubt the best friend."

I grin. And when he turns back to Amy and hugs her again, I don't feel like I'm on the outside looking in.

"God, I'm so glad you're OK," he says. "Don't go into the woods on your own like that again, OK?"

Amy leans into him. "I'm never going into those woods again if I can help it."

Twenty-six

Everyone wants to know what happened to Amy in the woods.

"Were you scared?" Cecily asks, eyes huge.

It's Monday and we're back at school. And even though I'm the one who found Amy, people are acting like it is my fault she got lost in the first place.

"Why were you in the woods again after the dance?" Danielle says, eyeing me like I'm some sort of forest freak.

"I was just on my way home," I lie.

Apparently Amy told everyone that she was going looking for me, and of course Mark told Steve about our search in the woods, and now the whole school knows.

I keep looking to Amy, waiting for her to jump in and defend me, but she doesn't say anything. Just stays close to Mark, like as long as she's by his side nothing bad can ever happen to her.

I'm so irritated at Cecily and Danielle and everyone asking me stupid questions that I almost don't notice my ring scar is burning again. And when I do, the first thing I do is look at Amy's. Her skin is smooth and calm. And instead of getting scared about what the burning means, I get angry. I'm on high alert for the rest of the day at school, waiting for something to go wrong. But nothing does. The day is remarkable only in its normality. On my way home, I look at Grandma Shirley's house and notice the curtains are closed. Which is weird for the afternoon. I'll go see her later. I know she'll make me feel better.

When I walk inside, my dad is sitting at the kitchen table with his head in his hands. "Dad?" I say, going tentatively up to him. My stomach is knotting and knotting like laces that can never be untied.

He turns to me with red-rimmed eyes.

"It's Grandma Shirley."

My parents won't let me go to the hospital to see Grandma Shirley.

"She isn't herself," says my dad. "She most likely had a stroke. She isn't able to speak just yet. It will only be upsetting for you, Bitsy." And he won't tell me anything else.

If I can't see Grandma Shirley, I only want to see one other person.

And I realize it isn't Skyler.

That when it matters, I need Amy.

She comes over right away. I don't know how she got here. Maybe Mark dropped her off. I'm just glad to see her.

"How is she?" Amy asks, hugging me tight.

"I still don't know the details," I say. "She fell down on her way to the bathroom but managed to call my mom. They think it was a stroke, but she's stable now."

"Oh, Bitsy," says Amy. "I'm sorry. That's so scary." We go into the kitchen and sit down at the table, like we have a million times before.

"Thanks for coming over."

"Of course," she says. "I'm here for you. And you know I love Grandma Shirley too. Maybe we can make cookies or something tonight? To bring to her when she's feeling better?"

"That's a good idea," I say.

Amy's phone buzzes and she looks down at it. "That's weird: it's Aunt Lily. She never calls. I'm just going to make sure everything is OK."

"Of course," I say, getting up to pour myself a glass of water. "She's probably worried about you after everything that happened."

"She still thinks I was pulling some sort of attention-seeking stunt," says Amy, rolling her eyes. But she answers the phone. I can't hear what Amy's aunt is saying, but I can hear that she's talking very fast. I turn and look at Amy, and I can't read her expression at all.

"What?" she says. And then again, more incredulously. "What? Is this a joke?"

Her eyes fill with tears and I immediately go to her, leaving the tap running.

"*What is it?*" I mouth.

She just shakes her head. "Really? Oh my god. I don't know what to say… Well of course I'm happy … it's just … a lot. Yeah, I'll come home soon. I'm just at Bitsy's… Of course I'm going to tell her."

She ends the call and puts her phone down with a shaky hand.

"Everything OK?" I ask. She's gone so pale she looks like she might pass out. I can't tell if it is good news or bad news, I just know that it is huge.

"My dad won some big poker tournament. Like won big. And now he's coming here. To Ember Grove. To stay."

In all the years we've been friends, I've never met Amy's dad. He's visited maybe three times, but Amy was always weird about those visits. She loves her dad, but it

235

isn't like they really know each other. And there's shame there too. I know she's embarrassed of him. So I've never pushed her about him, never made her talk about him when she didn't want to. I just always tried to make her feel like she belonged here. More than belonged. Like she was part of my family.

Now, the day that my grandma goes to hospital, she finds out that her dad has won big, and is coming here. As Amy said: it's a lot.

She's still staring at her phone, like it might bite her or burst into flames.

"Aunt Lily said he'll be here in two days. Apparently the poker tournament was in Milan. I didn't even know he was in Europe." She doesn't look up as I turn off the tap, still staring wide-eyed at her phone.

"That's great news," I say, but it sounds hollow even to my ears.

That snaps Amy out of it. "What a weird week," she says, shaking her head. "I just can't believe it. It isn't that I don't want to see him – of course I want to see him, of course I'm happy – it's just a lot to process, you know?" She shakes her head again. "Sorry. I'm here to make you feel better, and now I'm going on about this."

I know she's waiting for me to say that it's fine. That I understand. That I'm here for her.

But I don't. Instead, a strange theory that has been bubbling inside of me bursts out.

"Something weird is going on between us," I say. "No, more than weird. Something is wrong. Between us. With us."

"Bitsy, what are you talking about?"

"I think ... I think we're cursed or something. Or definitely linked. I don't think good things can happen to us at the same time any more. I think when good things happen to you ... bad things happen to me."

"Bitsy, I say this with a lot of love, but that is batshit."

"It isn't!" My voice is shrill. "Think of our scars! They link us, somehow. And the proof is there."

I finally tell her what I've noticed. How that when things go well for her, they go badly for me.

"And now the worst thing in the world is happening to me and, Amy, I need you to give something up. Please. For our friendship. For me."

"You're saying that you want things in my life to go to hell, so good things can happen to you?"

"No, of course not. I mean, not exactly. I'm just saying there's been a clear correlation."

"I think you're exhausted and stress is getting to you and making you unstable. Listen, I don't deny that weird things have been happening. You've convinced me of that much. But the idea that our fortunes are linked and when good things happen to me, bad things happen to you … I don't believe that. I'm sorry, but I don't. And I definitely don't appreciate you telling me all this when I find out my estranged dad might make an appearance and stick around for a while. Do you realize how messed up that is?"

"What I realize is how messed up it is that your dad only won his tournament because Grandma Shirley had a stroke!" I snap. "And who knows what else has to go wrong for me for things to keep going right for you?"

"Bitsy, I'm worried about you," says Amy, and the patronizing tone of her voice unravels something inside of me.

"You aren't! You don't give a shit about me! Because if you did, you'd be listening to me. Get out. Go find your perfect boyfriend."

"You know my life isn't perfect! You know that more than anyone," she says. "And I hate to be the one to break it to you, Bitsy, but sometimes shitty things happen to good people. How else do you explain everything that happened to me when I was little? Don't you think I wanted to blame the whole world? Sometimes life sucks. There isn't an explanation for it."

"Well this time there is an explanation!"

"You are being ridiculous," she says.

"I'm not! You always call me ridiculous in that patronizing way, like you think you are so much better than me, and you're not. My grandma is sick and maybe dying and I swear it has something to do with your dad coming home. Don't you think the timing is weird?"

"It's a coincidence, Bitsy," says Amy, with a pitying smile that I hate. "And you know what? For all your talk about what a bad friend I am, you are being a pretty terrible friend to me right now. My dad is finally succeeding at something. And he wants me back in his life. I don't have my mom, and I know my dad isn't perfect, but he's the only one I've got, and if I can have him in my life, I'm not going to mess that up. Why can't you understand that?"

"Because I'm not happy he's back! I want him to stay away so my grandma gets better! That is how this works! Can't you see?"

"You are unbelievable. If you really think that then you are both delusional and the most selfish person I've ever met. And I don't want to talk to you for a long time. I hope Grandma Shirley gets better, you know how much I love her, but I also know it has nothing to do with my dad."

"I'm not selfish! You are the one being selfish!"

But Amy isn't listening to me. She's putting on her coat and walking out of the door and not looking back.

Twenty-seven

I run into the woods.

Through the orchard, past trees I know so well, and then into the arms of the woods themselves. The woods welcome me, the trees stroking me with sharp branches as I run, leaves crunching underfoot. I don't keep my feelings bottled up. I howl like an animal, all my fear and anger pouring out of me. And the woods drink it up.

More, I can almost hear them say. *Give us more.*

And so I do. I keep crying, keep running. My sweat and tears mingle and drip onto the forest floor. *It isn't fair,* I think. *Amy isn't being fair. Why hasn't she given something up for me?* The thoughts propel me forward, deeper and deeper into the woods. I'm not paying attention to where I'm going. I'm following the call of the woods, going where they lead.

It is only when my toe catches on a root and I go sprawling that I realize I haven't even put on shoes. I lie on the ground for a moment, catching my breath, staring up at pieces of sky through the trees.

And then I hear it. The sound of water lapping against the shore.

Lake Lost. I've found it again, right when I need it most. I stagger to my feet and follow the sounds of the lake, and when I burst through the trees, the glassy stillness beckons me closer.

I keep walking until I'm ankle deep in the water and I can feel it soothing my sore and scraped feet. Only then do I stop, listening to the sound of the woods. The sound of my breathing, each intake of air a sharp burst in my lungs.

The lake ripples, only slightly, and I get the feeling that someone is watching me. I turn, quickly, to face the shore.

Skyler is standing there, watching me with that vaguely amused expression she seems to always have. "Little Bits! What's the emergency? You ran past me so fast you didn't even see me here."

Was she there? I could have sworn the lake shore was empty when I arrived.

I watch her a little warily, still trying to catch my breath. Still trying to calm my heart. I realize, with sharp and sudden clarity, I didn't run into the woods hoping to find Skyler this time. I wanted to be here alone. But maybe she can help, maybe she can make me feel better. Maybe she'll understand. "My grandma is sick. Really sick."

I don't know what I'm expecting, but it isn't for Skyler to shrug and roll her eyes. "Such is the nature of the old."

I frown. Who responds like that when someone says their grandparent is sick? "That's pretty harsh."

"It is true. The truth is often harsh."

"She's my grandma. You know how much she means to me."

"Even the most beloved of grandmas die eventually. Everyone does. Well. Almost everyone." Her eyes glint. And she grins, teeth sharp. "Your grandma never asked for anything, you know? It was your grandpa who was chosen that year at their Revelry."

Something about her widening grin makes me take a small step back in the lake.

"What are you talking about?"

Skyler shakes her head. "You haven't figured it out yet, have you? Even after all that's happened? Not as bright as I thought, Little Bits."

My vision goes a bit blurry at the edges and then very bright, almost as if I'm standing in an over-exposed photograph. I thought Skyler could give me answers, but I think Skyler *is* the answer.

Then I ask her the question that keeps buzzing around my head, louder and louder until it is all I can hear. "Why did you come looking for me? That first night?"

"I told you: I was curious about the girl who broke Revelry rules. And now that you're here, now that we're back where it all began..." She gestures to Lake Lost. "I'll admit to you that I thought you were the sacrifice. Someone has to be." Her grin grows sharper. "But it looks like you are something else."

All the air that I've just breathed in leaves me in a whoosh. I stand frozen and trembling, like a rabbit caught in a trap.

And I remember. I remember everything.

Emerging from the woods, after resting by the tree, after the dancing, and going back to the lake. Everyone gathered, turning to look at us.

The atmosphere changing. What had been a party, a celebration, turning into something sinister.

"What do we have here?" A voice from the centre of the crowd. It's the girl with silver hair, her eyes glittering behind a mask. "Two Revelry stowaways?"

Her voice carries on the wind; it is as clear as if she was standing right next to us. "Want to prove yourself, do you?"

Amy stepping closer to me. "Bitsy, what is she talking about?" She's nervous for the first time that night.

"We'll leave," I say, as loud as I can, but my voice comes out small and squashed.

The girl begins to hum and everyone else hums too: it is that song, that song I can't forget.

Being pushed, gently but firmly, until we're so close I could touch her. Her eyes glittering with a dark mania behind her mask.

"Lucky for you," she says, "we've got just the thing for you to prove that you are welcome at this Revelry." She steps aside with a flourish, revealing a circle of fire. In the centre is a pile of rocks, barely visible through the flames. It is almost as if the flames are protecting the rocks. She stares straight at me.

"Only the bravest would dare to sneak into a Revelry that isn't their own. The rocks in the centre have been piled there by Revellers who walked through the flames, as is tradition. Since you have come to a Revelry that is not your own —"

a collective inhale of disgust from the crowd — "it is only fair that you too face this."

The rock offered to me. The lake lapping against the shore. The fire burning brighter, higher. The very air around us crackling with energy. With yearning. My hands staying at my side. My arms so stiff I don't think I could lift them even if I wanted to.

And I don't want to.

"One can't reject a Revelry dare," she says, and her tone is light but her words are heavy.

"I'll do it," Amy says suddenly, her arm whipping out like a snake striking. She grabs the rock and it must be heavier than it looks because she staggers a bit under its weight. It's black as obsidian.

"Ember Grove Revellers," the masked girl says to the crowd, "do we accept her as a stand-in?"

The crowd roar their approval.

"Do it now," the girl says, firelight reflected in her eyes. "Before the lake and woods demand more."

Before I can try to stop her, before I can say that I'll go, or that it is stupid and neither of us need to do anything, Amy darts forward, the rock in her hands, her tie-dyed toga billowing out behind her, towards the fire circle.

I don't know how they expect her to get through it. The fire is waist high, and although it's contained, it's spitting sparks. Amy walks around it, clearly looking for a place where it's easier to slip through. But it's a solid wall of flames.

She starts to back up, and for a moment I think she's changed her mind, she's not going to do it, and I breathe a sigh of relief. But then. She charges forward, a look of fierce determination on her face, and with dawning horror I realize she's going to try to leap over the fire. She knows how to dance, after all. All the hours of choreography and rehearsals. She knows how to trick gravity. How to perform.

And for a moment, she's airborne, one leg extended in front of her, the other out behind, arms with the stone forward, hair streaming back, toga flying out.

And in the split second that she's in the air, that she's flying, my stomach unknots itself because I shouldn't have been worried: it's Amy, she can do this, she can do anything. I should have known she'd be able to leap over the fire.

But then, just as she's about to land, about to come back to earth and triumphantly place the stone on top of the cairn in the centre, a spark jumps up and catches the back of her toga – which isn't really a toga at all but a cheap tie-dyed sheet that isn't made to withstand even a little bit of heat – and she must feel it, because she glances back and her face changes, fierceness turns to fear, and she falls.

Falls hard.

Her head lands on the pile of stones, scattering them, and I hear the crack of her head hitting one of the rocks, and she doesn't move.

And suddenly, suddenly, the spark on the edge of her toga flares to life, and is climbing, climbing, getting closer to her legs, closer to her skin, closer to her. Her dress is on fire and she's lying in a pile of rocks, and nobody is doing anything ... and without thinking, I am running, and I am not trying to jump over the flames, I am running through them.

My own toga lighting up.

But Amy jumped into this fire for me, and I'll do the same for her. I don't slow down; I grab her under her arms; I pull her through the other side of the flames.

The lake is right there.

Water, shimmering and cold, and I pull her into it, screaming as I feel the fire go from my toga to my skin, and I'm burning burning burning, and then we're in the lake, falling falling falling.

Right before our heads go under, Amy's eyes fly open and then we're in the water, but I'm still burning and there are flames all around us, they've followed us, we're still encircled in flames, and I take a deep breath and I go deeper under, pulling Amy with me, away from the flames. My head smacks something hard and for a moment I think I might pass out. But no, I can't. I have to hold onto Amy. We have to get out of the lake.

We arise spluttering and shuddering from the lake, and someone is there with a blanket, covering us, warming us.

Our togas are charred black and soaking wet, but our skin is unmarked.

I know I was burned though. I felt it.

Most of the crowd have pulled away, giving us space, but they are watching us. The masked girl is watching us closest of all.

"I dropped the rock," Amy says. Her teeth are chattering.

"The stupid rock doesn't matter," I say. "Are you OK?"

She nods. "Are you OK?"

I nod.

The masked girl's voice echoes out. "The Revelry demands what it demands. And you will pay. One way or the other." She's grinning, teeth sharp and glinting. And the humming starts again, so much humming... That sound, get it out of my head, get it out, get it out...

"You!" I gasp. "You were the one who made us go into the fire circle!"

Skyler smiles. "Oh, Little Bits, I thought you would never remember. And I wish I could tell you I was sorry. But you broke the Revelry rules: it was only right." She laughs, her mouth wide open, showing all of her teeth. The clouds shift and the sun is so bright I squint for a moment, and the shadows all around us seem to come alive. "These woods like you, I can tell. The lake does too. You've given the woods a taste of you, of your fear and your tears, and now they are hungry for more."

I step back, deeper into the lake.

Nobody knows where I am.

My heart begins to beat against my ribs like a frightened bird in a cage.

"There's always a sacrifice, and it would have been

poetic, in a way, if it was you. Your family's apple trees, where do you think they came from? The woods gifted those trees to your family. But at a cost."

She comes closer, and I feel the sense that she's herding me, hunting me, and I try to stand my ground. I know her, don't I? But every instinct is screaming at me to run. To get far from her. "A boy was buried alive at your grandmother's Revelry and I oversaw it all. Who do you think threw the first fistful of dirt?"

I raise my own hand to my mouth, horror rising like bile in my throat. "No!"

"Oh, your precious grandmother didn't dirty her hands," she says, still grinning, grinning, grinning. "But she stood by and let your grandfather do it. She didn't try to stop him. She knew what he was doing. Your grandfather was so *hungry*. So ambitious. The Revelry answers the loudest call. And your grandfather wanted his land to be fruitful – and the land demanded something in return. The boy was pushed, the dirt was thrown and then the apples came."

The apples came after the Revelry, those were Grandma Shirley's words. *Oh, Grandpa Alfred, what did you do?*

"It isn't always a death," she says with a satisfied smirk that chills me to the bone. I remember all those names, the people who disappeared, the ones like Florence

Lonsdale who got an obituary, and the ones who simply melted away between the summer night and the dawn of the fall. What happened to them? "Sometimes it is a promise. A secret. A heart."

At the word heart, the childhood rhyme plays in my head again. The one we used to skip rope and play hop-scotch to.

Seven trees for seven wishes
Seven hearts for seven kisses
Seven deaths for seven dreams
Seven stitches in seven seams
Try to jump from six to eight
Because seven is where you'll meet your fate

Maybe it was always more than a nursery rhyme. Maybe it was a warning.

Skyler keeps talking. "But every year the Revelry demands something, and in exchange it gives. These woods were here long before Ember Grove's buildings were built, and they will outlast everyone and everything. And this year, the Revelry wanted something from you. I wonder, did your little friend – the one with the purple hair, the one who shines so bright – did she whisper a wish to bind you two? Is she not ambitious? Does she not want more than life has given her? Does she not want to be a star?"

"*You* did this. You cursed us."

Skyler shakes her head. "I wish I had that power. But I do not. You cursed yourself, you see. You began to believe it. You made it so."

She steps closer still. The trees seem to be coming closer too, the lake lapping at our knees. "Belief has power. And you, Bitsy Clark, are brimming with belief in all things Ember Grove."

She's right. I *do* believe in Ember Grove. I believe in my woods. And I believe they would never hurt me. Not now, or ever.

"The woods need someone to do their bidding. And the Revelry needs someone to lead it. I volunteered, my year. And I loved it. Dare I say, I revelled in it. I didn't want it to end. I wanted to run the Revelry for ever." Her voice drops. "Or so I thought."

She looks up at me again, her eyes sharp, her mouth quirking like she's got a secret that she can't hold in any longer. "I promised the woods I would stay. And in exchange they granted me what anyone – everyone – would want. They gave me youth. Endless youth."

I begin to shiver. "How ... how old are you?"

Her face darkens. "It doesn't matter. I'm one with the woods now. And you." Her eyes light up like a struck match. "You can be too. You can stay in your beloved woods for ever."

"I don't want that."

"Everyone will watch you the way they watched me at the Revelry. You will command their attention like nobody else."

"Why me?" I whisper.

"Because you love these woods like I do. You will make sure the tributes are paid. The sacrifices are made. You will do what it takes. You have what it takes. Say yes, Bitsy. And you will stay young."

"What will happen to you?"

"I'll be released from my promise to the woods. To the Revelry. It must be willingly given. You must say you want to take my place. The woods want this, Bitsy. Can't you feel it? The woods want this. They want you."

I look around at the trees and the sky and the lake. I breathe in the cold, crisp air.

And I know.

These are my woods, but they would not want to trap me like this.

"No," I say. "Skyler, I'm sorry, but no." My voice is firm, but I feel like I might crumble. Why did I trust her?

"The Revelry needs someone. And I want to leave Ember Grove. I want to leave the woods!" Her voice crescendos into a shout and her chest is heaving. "I want to see the sea. I want to climb mountains and lie under the desert sun. I have given enough to the Revelry. Enough to the woods."

"That is not my problem," I say. "I'm sorry that you can't leave." And I am. "But I'm not taking your place."

"No?"

"No."

"You can't say no to me. No to the woods."

"The woods aren't asking. *You* are." I throw the words like a weapon, and see them land. She gasps but then her eyes sharpen.

"And I am the voice of the woods!" Her voice is shrill, more piercing than I've ever heard it, and her mirrored eyes are wild. "I am the voice and the hands. Without me the woods—"

"The woods will be fine without you," I say. "You've trapped yourself here. You made the woods a promise they didn't ask for. But it is a promise all the same, and one you cannot break. Do not blame this on my woods." I raise my voice. "You are a *blight* on my woods."

Skyler flashes her teeth at me and leans so close I can feel her breath on my face.

"You asked, once, why I came for you instead of your friend. And now I will tell you the truth." She pauses and then looks down at me with so much disdain that

I flinch. "Because you are weak. I knew you would fall for flattery. I could see that you were starved of it."

She's sneering at me now. Skyler, who I thought saw me, truly saw me, is sneering at me.

"You will never be anyone special. You will never do anything of consequence. And I will make sure of it."

I hear someone calling my name.

Someone is coming for me. I'm going to be OK.

And I don't know if she hears the voice too, but she moves quickly, grabbing my wrist and holding on tight and pulling me deeper into the lake. It's over our knees now. "You think these woods belong to you, but really, you belong to them."

"Let go!" I struggle to get free, but her grip is like steel and I'm so focused on unclasping her fingers from my wrist that when she does let go, I stumble back, and then she shoves me in the chest. Hard. I fall, and I'm in the water now, spluttering and trying to get up.

"If you will not accept what I offer, if you will not take my place, then I will give you to the woods anyway. And maybe they will reward me for it."

And then she's holding me down.

Holding me under the water.

I'm a good swimmer, but this isn't swimming. I thrash, my head scraping the pebbles beneath my head, and this is not what the woods want, not *my* woods. This is not what the lake wants. I don't care what happened at the Revelry.

I'm struggling as hard as I can, kicking out, but her hands are pressing on my windpipe and through the dappled water I can make out her piercing eyes, so pale, watching as she drowns me, and then my vision starts to go and my chest hurts – it *hurts*.

And then she's off of me.

I splutter up out of the water, hands to my neck, gasping for air.

Amy is standing behind Skyler's slumped-over body, a rock in her hand.

She looks at me with fire in her eyes.

"My ring scar burned."

Twenty-eight

Amy drops the rock in the lake and reaches for my hand.

I'm shaking all over, but I can stand.

"Are you OK?" she says, eyes wide and worried.

"I think so. Thanks to you." My voice catches, but I swallow. I have to stay strong. We have to see this through. I squeeze her hand three times: one long, two short, and she does it back.

"What do we do with her?" she says, jutting her chin towards Skyler. She's slumped on the shore, half-in, half-out of the water. It is strange seeing her like this, so vulnerable. So … human.

I'm scared – frightened of what she became, of what she claimed to be. And at the thought of what she tried to take from me. Part of me wants to push her under until it is truly done.

But. "We can't leave her."

Together Amy and I drag the girl I thought was my friend out of the lake and back onto the shore and lay her gently on the sand. Her hair is matted with blood, but she's breathing.

"What now?" Amy's voice is anxious. "Should we take her to a hospital? To my aunt?"

But Skyler needs what only the woods can offer.

I look into the trees and speak, my voice clear and loud. "Release her."

A cloud of crows rises up out of the trees and flies at me and Amy. Amy shrieks and moves closer to me, but we don't back down. The birds fly on.

"I do not take her place," I say, and then I gently, so gently, push a strand of bloodied hair behind Skyler's ear. "But all the same I demand she is released. She has paid the Revelry tithe over and over again. Brought bodies and secrets and promises. But no more."

"Who are you talking to?" Amy whispers.

I ignore her and keep speaking to my woods.

"The Revellers will come and pay tribute in song and dance and laughter. But no sacrifices. No bargains."

The wind keens and the sound of hundreds of trees creaking echoes like bones scraping together. Still, I stand. I grab Amy's hand.

"I know it was not the woods who cursed me. Not you, not even Skyler. I cursed myself, and I am the only one who can break the curse. You saw the dark side of my heart." My voice breaks. "The curse was a reflection of my fears. I no longer have those fears. Things may change, sometimes for the worse, and sometimes for the better, but this —" I hold up Amy's hand — "this friendship will never truly break. But our curse will. I break it now." I hold Amy's hand tightly, and my voice is loud, and as I say the words the ring scar on my hand burns burns burns like it never has, glowing white, and then suddenly the pain stops.

The woods are silent.

The only sound is my own breathing.

Amy squeezes my hand three times, and as she drops it I notice her scar has changed and so has mine. No longer a circle, no longer a ring, just two smooth lines on the inside of our fingers, like an equal sign.

Then Amy gasps. "She's gone!" She points to a pile of clothes in front of us. Skyler's clothes.

I gaze into the woods. Looking for a sign of Skyler.

And then I see her broken-mirror eyes…

The fox with the broken-mirror eyes comes closer. It has reddish fur, but silver markings on its tail the colour of Skyler's hair.

"Is that…?" Amy's voice trails off.

The fox flicks its tail. Its face looks like Skyler's still, somehow.

I crouch down near the fox. I am not afraid.

"You're released," I say, holding out my hand. "The woods release you."

The fox that was once Skyler presses its nose to my hand gently. And I know she's saying sorry. Saying thank you.

I don't forgive her. Not when she tried to trap me. Not when she tried to drown me.

But. Skyler gave me something that I'll never forget.

She made me see that I am something special. She showed me that I shine.

"Leave while you can," I say.

The fox disappears into the woods. And I know I won't ever see Skyler again.

Amy and I walk back to my house in the twilight.

When we get to the orchard, I pause. I know now what this cost. And I know now that I don't want it. That the unspoken expectation that I will join the family business will never be met.

"I think I'm in shock," Amy says.

"I'm just glad you arrived when you did," I say. "How did you find me?"

She glances over at me. "I was on my way home when

my ring scar started to burn. And I knew, I just knew, that something bad was happening to you. And I ran – oh, Bitsy, I've never run so fast – I ran back into those woods that I swore I'd never go into again. And this time they led me straight to you. The woods wanted me to save you. I really believe that."

"I do too," I say softly.

"Do you still believe that if good things happen to me, they won't for you? That there's only enough good fortune for one?"

"It feels like that, sometimes," I admit.

"It feels like that for me too, you know? For the longest time it felt like you had everything, and I was, like, the little orphan friend, clinging on for scraps."

"It's never been like that. I can't imagine my life without you. You make my life so much better."

"You make my life better too. You always have." Then she smiles. "We should go visit Grandma Shirley tomorrow. We'll sneak in if we have to. I'd like to see her."

I'm filled with warmth. That's my Ames: confident she can get what she wants, and looking out for me too.

"That's a good idea," I say.

Amy looks at me carefully. "You don't still think my dad coming to stay with me is going to mean something bad happens to you, do you?"

I shake my head. "Not any more. And maybe not ever. Like you said, a weird thing happened to us. But it's finished now." And it is. Skyler is gone. The woods have released their hold on her, and on me. I'll always love my woods, but I'll never give them that kind of power over me again. "Thanks for saving me."

"I'll always come for you," Amy says, "just like I know you'll always come for me."

"Always."

"But, Bitsy?"

I look up at her tone.

"Let's stay out of the woods for a while."

The wind blows through my hair. I turn to look at the woods, and I swear they look back at me with something like pride.

"We're girls from Ember Grove. We have nothing to fear from our woods."

Acknowledgements

This book took me a long time to write and has gone through many iterations.

Once upon a time it featured a tricksy sea god who then turned into a pyromaniac and then turned into a mysterious boy living in the woods, who of course eventually became Skyler with the broken-mirror eyes. But all that time, the heart of the story belonged to Bitsy and Amy. It has always been a book about the power and complexities and beauty of female friendship, and I hope that it resonates with readers.

This book wouldn't exist without the support of a whole team of incredible people.

Thank you to my agent, the unparalleled Claire Wilson at RCW, for never giving up hope on this book and always believing in me. Thank you for everything.

I'd also like to thank Sam Coates and Safae El-Ouahabi at RCW for their support, as well as Miriam Tobin, who offered excellent early feedback. And thank you to Emily Hayward Whitlock at the Artists Partnership for her support.

Huge thank you to the wonderful team at Walker Books, I am so proud to be a Walker author. Thank you to Annalie Grainger, who first saw something in my initial idea and helped shape it, and was patient and supportive while I figured out the type of story this was. You are equally kind and brilliant, and I feel very lucky to have worked with you! Thank you to Non Pratt, who came in to the editorial process at a time when I felt like I'd lost my way and guided me back to the heart of the story and brought out the very best of it. This would not be the book it is without you, and I'm so grateful for your wisdom and insight and editorial brilliance. Thanks for helping make it a book that I'm proud of.

Thank you as well to Miranda Baker for the copy edit and Louise Millar for doing the typesetting.

I am grateful to the amazing Walker PR and marketing teams, especially Rosi Crawley, Ellen Abernethy, Lizz Skelly, and John Moore.

I am absolutely obsessed with the cover and the design of the book and have to thank designers Maria

Soler Canton and Maia Fjord for the brilliant concept, and of course illustrator Leo Nickolls for his stunning, incredible artwork.

Across the pond I'd like to thank David Levithan at Scholastic for his ongoing support and editorial insight, belief in me as an author, and for bringing *The Revelry* to the US.

The Revelry is a book about female friendship, so I would be remiss not to thank all of the incredible women in my life that I am lucky enough to count as friends. For Fay and Janou, to whom the book is dedicated, thank you for always being there for me and for all of the years we spent playing elaborate imaginary games – those shaped me as a person and as a writer. The funny thing is, *The Revelry* focuses on a complicated friendship, and our friendship has always been straightforward and effortless, but I still couldn't imagine anyone better to dedicate a book about friendship to.

To the women who knew me when I was a teenager and still mean so much to me – Coco, Emily, Katie Q, and Christina. To my Davis girls, Jess, Chlo, Abbie, and Jules, thank you for the memories and the joy and for always being there. To the friends I found in my twenties and became friends for life, Jeni and Dyna. And to the cohort of amazing women writers who I adore and admire – Cat, Kiran, Anna, Kate, Krystal, Samantha, Alwyn, Laure, Holly, Abi, KWoo, and Roshani. Special thanks to Holly Bourne, Krystal Sutherland, Cat Doyle, and Melissa Albert for their support for this book and offering such generous quotes – it means so much.

Thank you as always to my amazing family spread out all over the globe. I'd like to especially thank my siblings, Jack and Jane, as well as my parents, Rob and Virginia.

And thank you to Kevin, for cheering me on through every draft, for never giving up hope that I'd finish this book, for being my partner in all things. I love you and can't imagine life without you.

And to my daughter, Evie. I'm grateful for you every day, and hope you find the kind of friends I have, and always know how loved you are.

"Smart and kind and wise"
Katherine Rundell

KATHERINE WEBBER

That year she found the power to be extraordinary.

With a grandmother from China and another from Ghana, fifteen-year-old Wing Jones is often caught between worlds. When tragedy strikes, she discovers an extraordinary talent she never knew she had. Wing's running could bring her family everything it needs. It could also keep Wing from the one thing she truly wants.

"I loved *Wing Jones*. And it makes you want to pull on your shoes and start running."

KATHERINE RUNDELL

"In her darkest time, Wing finds her own strength. I fell in love with *Wing Jones* and you will too."

LAINI TAYLOR

Reiko loves the endless sky and electric colours of the Californian desert. It is a refuge from an increasingly claustrophobic life of family pressure and her own secrets.

Then she meets Seth, a boy who shares a love of the desert and her yearning for a different kind of life. But Reiko and Seth both want something the other can't give them. As summer ends, things begin to fall apart. But sometimes a broken heart is all you need to set you free…

"Magical, complex and nuanced."

Sara Barnard

Katherine Webber is originally from California but currently lives in London. She loves an adventure, whether in a book or in real life. Her YA novels include *Wing Jones* and *Only Love Can Break Your Heart*, but she also co-writes younger series *Sam Wu* (Egmont) and *Dragon Mountain* (Simon and Schuster) with her husband as Katie and Kevin Tsang.

@kwebberwrites
@kwebberwanders
@WalkerBooksUK
@WalkerBooksYA